Dragonflies

SUPRIYA PARULEKAR

Copyright © Supriya Parulekar 2024
All Rights Reserved.

ISBN
Paperback 979-8-89610-290-8
Hardcase 979-8-89632-746-2

Contents

One 5
Two. 13
Three 22
Four 30
Five 35
Six 38
Seven 47
Eight. 53
Nine 60
Ten 64
Eleven. 70
Twelve. 73
Thirteen. 78
Fourteen 82
Fifteen. 93

Contents

Sixteen 98

Seventeen 105

Eighteen 107

Nineteen 115

Twenty 120

Twenty One 126

Acknowledgement 271

O_{ne}

The young girl in the waiting room of Dr. Keshav Kulkarni's clinic was an epitome of patience. In her hands was a rosary. The beads sparkled as they caught the afternoon sun. They slipped between her fingers, smoothly with finesse and elegance. The young receptionist with a pleasant smile, asked if she would like tea or coffee, which the girl politely turned down. This girl was Tania Rana, stepsister to Sonya Rana, the reigning queen of Bollywood. Tania was highly protective of her elder sister.

Tania studied in Canada but when visiting home, she accompanied Sonya everywhere, even to her sessions with the therapist, Dr. Kulkarni. Today Sonya's session had spilled over an hour, but Tania had not moved an inch from her seat. Nearby, one of the patients had opened the mandala colouring book and began sketching.

Dr. Kulkarni's consulting room reflects his personality-filled with eclectic art, shelves lined with books on psychology and philosophy and a collection of mandala colouring books that he used as a conversation starter. Sky-blue wallpaper formed the backdrop for his desk. Dr. Kulkarni believed in using colour as therapy, hence the mandala colouring books placed at in the waiting room, encouraged his patients to indulge in a colouring activity while they waited.

"Hello, Sonya. I am glad you could make it today. How have you been feeling since our last session?" Dr. Kulkarni had a warm, engaging demeanour that put his patients at ease. He had salt-and-pepper hair, suggesting both experience and vitality. He sported a well-groomed beard and wore classic frame, perched on the bridge of his nose.

Sonya put down the colour pencil and sighed. "To be honest, not great. I feel...heavy like there's this weight on my chest." Sonya looked away.

"Can you tell me more about that?" the doctor asked in a gentle tone.

"I can't seem to shake this sadness. Some days, I don't even want to get out of bed." Sonya twirled a finger around a strand of her hair and tugged at it. It was as if she wanted to experience physical pain, the doctor noted.

"That sounds tough. Have there been any specific thoughts or feelings that stand out for you?" Dr. Kulkarni was in his late fifties.

"I have thoughts about not being here anymore. It's like a sad song stuck in my head. I am afraid...it doesn't scare me." Sonya looked at him, eyes clouding with sadness.

"I appreciate your honesty, Sonya. Let's talk some more about these thoughts. When you say you think about not being here anymore, what does that look like to you?" Dr. Kulkarni leaned forward in his chair.

Sonya looked at him, tugging strands of her hair, nearly plucking it out. "I just feel like it would be easier for everyone if I wasn't around. Sometimes I think about how to make it happen." Her voice trailed off with the thoughts in her head.

Dr. Kulkarni nodded in an understanding way. "Maybe you are feeling overwhelmed right now. It is crucial that we take these feelings seriously. Can you share with me if you have a plan or any specific thoughts about how you might do that?"

Sonya answered promptly, without hesitation. "I want to feel real pain. I want to put an end to this throbbing pain that seems to claw my insides. My mind plays games with me, trapping me in this perpetual darkness." She appeared terrified.

Dr. Kulkarni listened in rapt attention as tears threatened to storm down Sonya's cheeks. Her eyes were a warm shade of blue. They were filling up with despair. Dr. Kulkarni walked around his desk and approached her with a box of tissue. There was a considerable gap between his desk and the couch meant for the patients. Sonya plucked a tissue but instead of using it, she began folding the ends, sniffling tears.

"Sonya, is there someone at home you can talk to or reach out to for support?" Dr. Kulkarni circled back to his desk. Sonya once again began to colour.

"I don't want to burden them with my problems." Sonya replied.

"It's okay to share what you are going through. Often people want to help but don't know how, and by sharing, you might find that they can offer support." Dr. Kulkarni waited for a reaction from Sonya, an acknowledgement but saw none coming.

"Sonya… are you sure you have told me everything?" Dr. Kulkarni leaned forward; confident his patient was keeping something to herself.

For the world, she was a diva, but here in his consulting room, Sonya Rana was a broken girl, helpless.

"I am transparent and honest with you, Doc." Sonya looked away, which confirmed doctor's suspicions.

"Sonya, are you willing to try some coping techniques? We can start with mindfulness and breathing exercises."

"That sounds okay, I suppose." Sonya nodded after giving it a thought.

"Sonya, try this to begin with. For one dark thought, think of a happy place. It won't be easy at first. You must train your mind to stop the thoughts from taking control."

Poring over the notes from the past sessions, Dr. Kulkarni noticed that Sonya's mental health was deteriorating. He twiddled his thumbs, wondering what more he could do for her.

"Additionally, I would like to work on a safety plan together, just to ensure you have steps to take if these thoughts become stronger."

This elicited a deep sigh from Sonya.

Sonya swiped at the tears with the back of her sleeve. "Doc, you are the only person I am honest with about my feelings, my thoughts, of course after Jay."

Dr. Kulkarni noticed a slight shift in her mood at the mention of Jay's name. A tinge of hope, perhaps! But her eyes clouded soon enough.

"Sonya, how are things between you and Jay?"

"Jay…and me…it's like I am in some kind of a beautiful dream from which I am afraid to wake up in case it ends," Sonya said dreamily.

"Hold on to that thought and tell me how it makes you feel?"

A range of emotions flitted through Sonya's face. Happiness lasted for a bit and once again her eyes clouded.

"I can't…"

"What are you afraid of, Sonya?"

"Afraid of losing the people I love. Afraid I might hurt them the way I am hurting. I destroy everything beautiful around me." Sonya had wandered off mentally in her thoughts.

"We can always give life an opportunity to surprise us, can't we?" Dr. Kulkarni was observing her closely. A vacant look flashed in her eyes.

"Let's talk about the nightmares. What's the intensity like?" To this question Sonya stiffened.

"Do you think your nightmares are connected to your childhood?"

"Doc, we have talked about it in many sessions. I have nothing to add."

Sonya snapped. Dr. Kulkarni realised her defences were up. Anger claiming her calm demeanour. He had lost the little window of opportunity he had to understand the real Sonya Rana.

"I want to go through it once more," Dr. Kulkarni persisted, confident that the roots of her depressed state of mind lay in her childhood which Sonya refused to share.

"Let us go back to the day your stepsister was born. You were six, am I right?" Dr. Kulkarni noticed the look of disconcertion cross her face. Last session, she had become edgy and refused to answer this question. Dr. Kulkarni knew he had to push if need arises.

Sonya bit her lip, agitation evident, and avoided eye contact. Sonya glanced at her watch. She got up abruptly to leave.

"I must go. Thanks for your time, doc."

Dr. Kulkarni did not try to stop the girl. Sighing, he leaned back, watching her leave. He turned to the screen, which showed the corridor outside.

Dr. Kulkarni was confident that his patient was hiding the most important part from her childhood, which had now festered into a painful boil. Sonya took comfort from that pain, hence clutched the memories closer, tighter.

∗ ∗ ∗

Tania got up and walked over to her sister, who had just emerged from the doctor's cabin. Sonya slid on the sleek aviators and wrapped her face in a scarf to avoid drawing attention to herself. Heads turned; curious eyes followed her as Sonya walked by.

Dr. Kulkarni watched the girls leave, with Tania's arm protectively around her sister's shoulder. They hugged as Tania looked at her with grave concern. She seemed to murmur something in her ear as Sonya nodded her head in affirmation. Next, Tania adjusted the scarf to cover Sonya's face, and then the two sisters walked out.

Dr. Kulkarni smiled, thinking to himself how lucky Sonya was to have a sister like Tania, a friend, a confidante.

Two

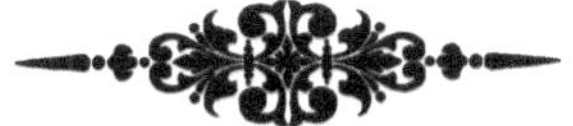

Sonya appeared exhausted as Tania helped her into the car, keeping a wary eye for paparazzi. She got in and drove off with Sonya, who leaned her head on Tania's shoulders.

"Exhausting session, huh?" Tania expertly manoeuvred the car through alleyways to avoid the paparazzi.

"Doc keeps prodding into my childhood. He doesn't understand that he wants me to dig up the muck. Those memories are like a sinkhole." Sonya shuddered inwardly.

Tania patted her hand comfortingly.

"I got you, Di. Nobody can force you to do things you don't want to."

Sonya sighed and squeezed Tania's hand.

"You must be tired. Why don't you take a short nap while I drive you home?" Tania's voice was soothing and gentle.

Sonya murmured "Hmm…" and lay back.

Tania had always been protective of Sonya, much to her mother's chagrin. Ramola tried hard to keep the girls away from each other. Ramola believed Sonya was a bad influence on her daughter.

Tania had come to understand that Ramola was jealous of Sonya as she was gorgeous and whenever they stepped out together, people ignored Tania and lavished their attention on the gorgeous Sonya.

Sonya had inherited her good looks from Meher, her birth mother. Sonya was tall with ginger-brown hair falling down her waist, a flawless complexion, a straight nose, and perfect cheekbones. Tania was of average height, had a button nose, brown eyes, freckles that had popped up in adolescence and made her face their 'forever' home, a curly mop of hair which she preferred to keep tied in a bun, and seemed to struggle with weight issues. She adored her elder sister and did not care about her mother's opinion. Tania went out of her way to keep her sister happy and comfortable.

"Hey T, what was the world up to while I was holed up in the doc's cabin?" Sonya asked, looking at the city passing by in a blur.

"You can never relax, can you? Anyway, your 'world' kept calling frantically." Tania tossed Sonya's cell at her as she manoeuvred the BMW in heavy afternoon traffic.

"Why torture the poor soul! You could have told him I was in my sessions with the doc," Sonya made a face.

"Not my monkey, not my circus." Tania shielded herself from the punch that came at her and giggled while Sonya dialled Jay's number.

Jay Malhotra, an MBA graduate, had joined his father's advertising firm fresh out of college. Jay was madly in love with Sonya but had never expressed his feelings to her, afraid that she might cut him loose.

Sonya's lips curved into a smile on remembering their first meeting. It was a crisp summer afternoon. Sonya was shooting for her debut movie and was put up in a hotel, in a remote place on the outskirts of Mumbai. Sonya ached for an ice cream and would have done anything to get one, had it not been for Jay's car parked outside her vanity van.

Jay had come to meet the producer hoping to bag the promotional campaign for Sonya's film. He got into his car, unaware of the fact that Sonya had managed to break in and was in the back seat. Five minutes into the ride, Sonya slowly sat up. Jay got the fright of his life as he dangerously swerved, nearly driving them both off the road. After heart-pounding anxious moments, he stopped and glared at her. Sonya was giggling in the back seat, her face buried in her palms.

"Are you crazy? Who the hell are you? And how did you manage to get into my car?" Jay yelled. He could hear his heart beating wildly.

Sonya slowly uncovered her face for Jay to see. Jay later described that moment to Sonya. It was surreal.

"I did not mean to startle you," Sonya said. "I am Sonya Rana..." She smiled at Jay, who seemed to have frozen in time.

"I know you...I mean... I just saw you on the poster..." Jay fumbled to get the right words but failed miserably.

"Listen, I don't want to stress you. It's hot outside and..."

"So, you broke into my car!" Jay was astounded and glad that the girl chose his car.

"No... let me explain. I just wanted to have an ice cream and the b**** trainer on set is not letting me have one," Sonya looked back, afraid Ramola's cronies would show up, finding her missing.

Jay was still not able to comprehend where this was going.

"Please... please, one ice cream and I am sorted." She looked like a little girl pleading for a toy.

"Do you have any idea how unsafe it is to get into a stranger's car? What if I were a serial killer?" Jay looked at *her through the rear-view mirror. What she did next surprised him.*

Sonya climbed into the front seat and put on the seatbelt.

"If you don't mind… I was feeling lonely back there. And to answer your question, my gut says you are not a killer but a saviour. Now, how about we get that ice cream?" Sonya winked at Jay, who looked at her in disbelief.

"I love how focused you are. It's my honour to ride with a star."

Since that day, Jay smuggled ice creams to her on her movie set.

"Next time… don't break into my car, okay?" He waved as she walked to the vanity van.

"Hello, baby…" Sonya crooned over the phone as Tania threw a smile in her direction.

Tania was happy that Sonya had finally found an anchor in life. Just thinking about what her sister had been through and how Ramola treated her like trash was traumatising. Tania had always acted as a shield, protecting her sis from the big bad world, and she continued to do so even today.

"Babe, where have you been? I was so worried," Jay had just stepped out of his office when he saw Sonya's name flash on his cell phone.

"I was with my therapist, and you know the sessions… so exhausting," Sonya yawned, bored. She sipped on the detox water that Tania passed to her.

"So thoughtful my little sis is. She knows exactly what I want and when I want," Sonya thought, glancing over at Tania, giving her a warm smile.

A thought struck her as she excitedly sat up. "Hey, T and I are going shopping. A bit of a retail therapy won't hurt. What say?"

Sonya always acted on impulse. She made plans based on her mood. If she was very happy, she would be cheerful for days. If her mood dipped, Sonya would stay in bed, and stare into nothingness, refusing to talk or meet anyone. Jay and Tania were not an exception.

Jay blew kisses at her through the phone as he heard Sonya and Tania shout in glee.

The girls shopped for every brand imaginable. Sonya had splurged lakhs of rupees on Tania and herself. Jay hauled the shopping bags from one store to another.

"I feel sated! There is no therapy like shopping," Sonya exclaimed, throwing her bags on the chair next to her. They sat down for an early dinner before heading home.

Tania looked at her sister fondly as she took off her glasses and scarf. She was gorgeous and precious. Tania made a vow to herself. She would do anything to shield her from the brutalities of the world.

A few moments later, they sipped on champagne and enjoyed caviar. Jay hugged Sonya, and they began to kiss. Tania groaned, making a face.

"You guys behave as if I don't exist!" Tania said exasperatedly.

The next moment, Jay let go of Sonya and moved towards Tania.

"I don't mind…" he said mischievously, moving closer towards Tania, gazing deeply into her eyes. "The more the merrier."

Tania, embarrassed, looked around wondering what Jay was up to.

"I… I did not mean that. You are getting me wrong," Tania stammered, looking over at Sonya for help, who was amused by the whole thing.

"What did you mean, sweetheart?" Jay murmured, his voice rich and suggestive as he stroked her cheek.

"Jay… don't you dare trouble my little sis," Sonya pulled Jay away from Tania.

Jay, laughing, turned to Sonya and exclaimed, "Wasn't that brilliant?"

Sonya grinned and kissed Jay. "If I knew I was getting a kiss from you, I can show you rest of my talents too." Sonya giggled while Tania pretended that the whole thing never happened.

Jay winked at a relatively relieved Tania and wrapped his arm protectively around Sonya.

"Hey Tania… sorry dear. You really fell for my act! I am too good, man… too good!" Jay said, in good humour.

Tania was still blushing with embarrassment. Tania had no social life, no friends. Her world revolved around Sonya. Ramola encouraged Tania to move out on her own, make new friends, but Tania stuck close to Sonya whenever she was home from Canada. Ramola hated Tania for being Sonya's shadow!

To cut off ties between the girls, Ramola sent Tania to the hostel when she was 10 years old while Sonya, at 16, was groomed for life in Bollywood. Ramola knew Sonya had the looks and capabilities to be a star just like Meher. She thought of this as a perfect opportunity to make money. Hence, after Raghav's death, Ramola sold off his business and moved to India. She couldn't sell the family house in New Jersey as it was bequeathed to Sonya by her father. Sonya refused to sell.

Sonya's mother, Meher, had walked out on Sonya when she was a toddler for a promising career in Hollywood.

Meher had a successful modelling career before marriage. She was ambitious and wanted to branch out into films, but her husband Raghav was conservative. The two fought and bickered but Raghav was adamant. He threatened to throw her out. Then, a frustrated Meher vented her anger on Sonya, keeping her hungry and crying. One day, Raghav left for India on a business trip, and Meher made the best of the opportunity. She believed she was not cut out for motherly duties. She left Sonya in day-care and went away to make a career for herself.

Raghav looked everywhere for Meher, even checked the local casting agencies. But no one had heard or seen the woman. Raghav waited for over a year for Meher to return, then married Ramola. Ramola had often narrated this story to the girls. Meher had disappeared, never to return.

The feeling of being abandoned and unwanted was deeply rooted in Sonya. She wondered if she ever came face to face with Meher, would it help the demons to go away?

Three

It was past midnight. Ramola had called the girls, but neither of the two had answered. Mentally preparing themselves to face the woman's wrath, the girls walked to their car. Tania was in the driving seat when Jay knocked on her window.

"Hey, sweets, thanks for looking after her," Jay smiled gratefully, pointing in Sonya's direction as she walked towards Jay's Ferrari.

"I love her too, dude," the smile on Tania's face quickly replaced with worry.

"Hey dude, if she is planning to ride with you, don't let her drive… come what may." Tania had not taken her eyes off her sister.

Sonya waved excitedly. Jay waved back.

"Don't worry. I promise you she is not getting behind the wheel…" Jay was too late.

Jay and Tania saw something red flash by them at high speed.

"Holy shit!" Jay exclaimed, hopping in alongside Tania who didn't give him time to close the door.

"My worst fears are coming true. Sonya… please don't do this," Tania murmured, drumming her fingers on the steering wheel.

Jay was frantically trying Sonya's cell.

"Do you think Sonya is going to answer your call? Why the hell did you leave her alone…? She is fragile… I told you…"

Frustration and anger evident in her voice, she knew Jay was not to be blamed, but she had to say something to keep from going insane with worry. Was Sonya having one of her episodes?

✳ ✳ ✳

Sonya, unmindful of the chaos she had caused was lip syncing to Taylor Swift's Anti-Hero; 'It's me, Hi…I am the problem it's me….' She accelerated and the car shot through the darkness. Before Sonya could comprehend what was happening, she was flying, the steering-wheel slipped and seemed to have a mind of its own. She could smell the burning tires and heard the screech as metal touched the ground. Was it her end? Why didn't she feel fear? Sonya felt empty.

✳ ✳ ✳

Tania pressed the accelerator, driving at a break-neck speed. It was past midnight, and the roads were relatively empty. What if Sonya was intercepted by the cops? Or, worse still, what if she met with an accident? God, please. Tania sent up fervent prayers.

Jay was scanning the roads on both sides. They were now on the Andheri flyover. The Sahara Star hotel was to Tania's right. For her, the hotel resembled a space ship whenever she travelled through.

An ambulance passed by them, its siren sounding ominous in the night. Tania skipped a heartbeat. Jay was staring right ahead at the police car and the crowd gathering in huge numbers.

Tania's heart was racing faster than the speedometer of her car. It had to be Sonya! What had happened to her? What had she done? Was she safe? Random thoughts ran through her mind. She came to a halt a few metres away from the blaring siren of an ambulance which had passed them a couple of minutes ago.

The sight before her left Tania gasping for breath. Jay was too shocked to react as he stared ahead, numb. His car was precariously perched on the ledge. Sonya was at the wheel, unconscious.

Tania took a long swig at the inhaler. Her breathing somewhat normalised. It was impossible to get Sonya out of this mess unnoticed. With the police and the press involved, she could see the headline flashed in the next day's newspapers and television news channels.

Additional Police Commissioner Arjun Deshmukh was passing by when he noticed the red Ferrari hurtle down the bridge, at high speed. The driver at one point seemed to have lost control and braked, causing the car to jerk and swerve. Arjun had seen sparks flying as the car careened over the ledge. For a moment there, he thought the Ferrari would hurtle down, taking the driver to his imminent death. Thankfully, it stopped as it balanced itself precariously on the narrow ledge. The danger had not passed yet. Arjun had immediately informed the control tower and asked for an ambulance and fire brigade. He rushed over to see whether he could be of help. The first thought that crossed his mind, 'must be a rich brat out on a joyride, endangering lives.'

Arjun was surprised to see a young girl behind the wheel. Her hair was splayed all over her face, making it difficult to know if she was conscious. It was two minutes into the accident, and already a crowd had gathered. He noticed spotted people filming the incident on their cell phones.

Arjun dispersed the crowd as a young girl and boy ran towards the car. Arjun intercepted.

"Excuse me… please stay back. Help is on the way," he tried to stop them from going ahead.

Arjun noted the girl was barely able to breathe. She removed an inhaler, took a deep breath, still gasping for breath.

"Sir… I am Tania Rana and the girl in the car…" pointing to the Ferrari, "is my sister, Sonya Rana," her words were barely a whisper. She was trembling in fear.

"The Sonya Rana…?" To that, the young girl nodded, anxiety and tension palpable.

This was front page news. Arjun looked around and spotted the regular journalists on this beat. They waved at him, signalling frantically, shadows outrunning them to the wreckage. They were werewolves, circling from all sides, closing in dangerously, following the scent, ready to kill.

Arjun knew it was difficult to retrieve Sonya from the wreckage, unnoticed, which her sister expected!

Sonya heard a buzzing sound start in her head. Were they bees? She tried to focus in the direction of the sound but felt disoriented. She opened her eyes and was surprised. They weren't bees but dragonflies. Sonya's mind travelled to her childhood where her father taught her to catch a dragonfly and hold its wings for a few seconds in order to tame them. Sonya tried to catch one, but soon realised her hands had gone numb. Next, she sensed ants crawling up her legs. Sonya screamed but it was a silent scream. The impact had sent her body into shock. Sonya heard her name being called. The voice was gentle and kind but seemed to come from miles away. Suddenly, she saw a bright light. *I must be dead*, she thought.

"Sonya… Sonya, if you are fine, nod your head." The same gentle and kind voice. Now coaxing her, urgency evident. Only if the voice knew what an ordeal it was to move even an inch.

Arjun had taken it upon himself to extricate the girl from the wreckage. With Jay's help, Arjun freed open the door that had jammed on impact. By the time he managed to open the front door, Jay had slid in and untied the seat belt, calling out to Sonya.

"Hey babes… don't worry, I will get you out of this mess."

Jay planted a kiss on her forehead. His gaze hovered on her face, checking for any injuries. Blood trickled down the side of her head. There seemed to be a deep wound as the hair was matted in one particular place, above her ear. Jay's handsome face creased with worry.

"Am I dead? Jay…what are you doing here?" Sonya frowned at Jay's concerned face.

They could hear the ambulance.

"I can't move my hands… can't feel my legs. I am flying." Sonya laughed deliriously and immediately winced in pain.

Arjun exchanged a concerned look with Jay.

"Ma'am, look at me. Help is near. We are now transporting you to the ambulance. Please calm down," Arjun made way for the paramedics who helped Sonya onto a stretcher.

Onlookers and the press alike, surrounded the trio, clicking pictures. The press wanted to know about the accident. Was Sonya drunk? Whose car was she driving? Who else was with her? Was she seriously injured? Would she be charged for driving under the influence? Was anybody else hurt?

Tania replied with a curt 'No comment' and entered the waiting ambulance along with Sonya and Jay.

"Sorry about your car!" Sonya made a sad face.

"We can get a new car, babe. You are precious." Those were the last words Sonya heard before she lost consciousness.

Four

Ramola paced the hospital corridor outside ICU where doctors attended Sonya. She was furious. What did this girl want from life? She was the reigning Diva of Bollywood. She had everything at her feet; beauty, money, fame, and success. Sonya was always a troublemaker and did not have to go far looking for some. What a mess she was in? Ramola thought to herself. The press was going crazy. They wanted details about the accident. They were hounding Ramola.

Jay was waiting a few paces away. He looked sick with worry. Ramola saw her daughter speaking to Jay, patting his shoulder, and smiling assuringly.

"This boy is to blame for this accident. Why let Sonya drive in the first place?" Ramola mumbled angrily.

"Mom... Sonya Di will be fine. It was no one's fault. Jay and I were talking when Di took off in Jay's car."

Ramola gave her a scathing look. She took Tania by her arm and dragged her to one corner.

"I had told you to bring Sonya home after her sessions, hadn't I? Can't you do one thing right? I can never depend on you, Tania," Ramola whispered angrily, casting wary glances around.

Tania struggled to free her arm from her mother's grip. "Mom, you are hurting me."

"What if anything happens to Sonya? Do you understand what repercussions this accident will have on her as an actor? Do you have the faintest idea? One scratch on her face or anywhere on her body and she is ruined." Ramola hissed, nostrils flaring with anger. A nerve on her forehead twitched as she pinned Tania with an angry look.

Tania jerked her hand away and looked pointedly at Ramola.

"I care about Di. I am not worried about her acting career," Tania hissed back.

"Fine, say goodbye to fancy college and the luxurious life you enjoy." Ramola's eyebrows knotted together.

"I feel you put too much pressure on Di. And I can survive a non-luxurious life." Tania felt disgusted for her mother's shallow thinking.

Ramola watched horrified and wondered if she really had given birth to this girl. She was completely smitten by Sonya. In spite of her best efforts to keep the girls away, they had found a way to bond with each other, and that surprised her.

"I have to find a way to keep the sisters apart," Ramola decided to herself.

The doctors treating Sonya approached them. Fortunately, she got away with bruises and a sprain in her wrist and neck, but they needed to keep her under observation for the night.

"I told you Di will be fine. You were unnecessarily getting worked up," Tania rushed into Sonya's room followed by Jay.

"You scared me, Di. Do you ever pause and think for a moment about what Jay and I go through with these daredevil acts of yours? Don't you love me? Why Di... why?"

Tania's quivering voice was enough to convey how much she was hurting at this moment.

Sonya's eyes filled with tears and she opened her arms for Tania who was angry and hurt. Jay patted her shoulder, nodded to forgive Sonya. Tania ran into her sister's arms. Jay too, joined them.

Ramola saw the sisters hug each other, laugh about the whole thing. She shook her head, wondering if her efforts had gone to waste.

After her husband, Raghav's untimely death, Ramola had the reins in her hands. The first thing she did was send Tania to Canada and relocate to India. Here she pushed Sonya into movies. It was a cakewalk for the girl as she was gorgeous and talented like her mom, Meher. Everything was going according to her plans until one day, Sonya staggered in drunk from a New Year's party. Ramola's dreams came crumbling down.

Sonya's drinking had increased over the days, and it became a cause of concern when she started holding up shoots. Ramola would find Sonya drunk and crying in her room. Instead of comforting her, Ramola reprimanded Sonya for her behaviour. Ramola then decided Sonya needed to see a therapist before the word got out and work stopped coming.

Ramola consulted, Dr. Keshav Kulkarni, the acclaimed therapist for Sonya. After a couple of sessions, there was a marked improvement in Sonya, and Ramola thought things will go back to normal.

Ramola had chalked out a life for both the girls, and she hated it when anything went wrong. Like now, when Sonya had started losing her grip on life. She had taken to drinking and popping pills as it pleased her.

From what Sonya did today, Ramola knew Sonya's mental state was fragile, and she needed extensive treatment. However, the lucrative offers coming her way and the money they brought were tempting. She had to pull Sonya out of this somehow; even if it meant she had to accompany Sonya on shoots, so be it! She would push her to the limits. Ramola walked into the room with a broad smile and fake concern.

Five

Arjun was thinking about Sonya Rana and her foolish attempt at achieving a cheap thrill last night as was said in the news. Was this true? Was this about thrill or something deeper? Arjun knew his readings about a person had never been wrong.

Arjun was a competent officer. His logical reasoning was appreciated by his peers and seniors. A trait inherited from his father, the late Manohar Deshmukh, who had been an efficient police officer of his times but the police job was not something Arjun had in mind. Arjun was patriotic. He would be the only child in his school dressed in an army uniform, waving India's flag during Independence Day celebrations. He always cherished a dream of wanting to join the army and serve his country.

Nothing happens according to plan, and Arjun had learned it the hard way.

That chilly morning, when Manohar Deshmukh had decided to take his life, little was he thinking about his ten-year-old son and his young wife whom he was leaving behind. He simply threw himself in front of the first train that came thudding down the railway tracks. What drove him to kill himself? His colleagues say it was frustration at the job. Others say he was being questioned about the possible encounter case he had assisted his senior cop with. In quest for the answers to his father's death, Arjun had joined the police service.

Arjun knew he was chasing ghosts in dark alleys and every time he thought he found answers, he drew up against a wall.

Sonya's case file worried him. He could see pain behind this fake smile Sonya put up for the world. Arjun was confident, if he dug deeper, he would uncover some dark secrets buried deep in her past. Arjun's police mind was telling him, it's a case of an accident caused by reckless driving. He should follow the normal necessary procedures and take steps to prevent it from happening again. He had sensed a strangeness in the younger sister. She needs to be watched, he convinced himself.

The rash driving, near-to-death collision was not an isolated incident. This was just the beginning, an onset of a tragedy waiting to happen. Unhappy people, unhappy minds! It was time to meet Sonya Rana. Arjun picked up the file and walked out to the waiting police jeep.

Six

Sonya was recuperating back home. Gaurav, her secretary for five years, cancelled her appointments for a week so that Sonya could rest well and recover from the traumatic incident. He now stood talking to Ramola in hushed tones outside Sonya's bedroom.

"Madam, there is no cause to worry. Sonyaji's dates will be accommodated in the next schedule."

Gaurav knew how worked up Ramola would get when Sonya missed her shoots.

"I don't understand why this girl is behaving like this! There is so much at stake here." Frustration was obvious in Ramola's voice as she ranted about Sonya's intrepid attitude.

Sonya's right arm was in a sling. She had hurt her shoulder, but fortunately, there was no fracture. She was given painkillers and sedatives and advised bed rest. Sonya had been sleeping since morning. She woke up, drowsy, and walked over to her closet. After a few seconds of shuffling things around, she found what she was looking for: a bunch of letters.

Sonya was now sitting on the bed with the letters strewn around her. She would pick one letter, glance through it and then do the same with others. She closed her eyes and a feeling of satisfaction washed over her. She replaced the letters in its hiding place and scrolled through her phone messages. While she was asleep, Jay had texted and called. She felt happy about Jay being in her life.

Jay and Tania were her only true support. Although Tania was younger, she was more mature, and Sonya at times blindly went with her decisions.

"Di, do things that you love. Don't worry about being judged. Don't allow anyone to walk over you." Tania would gently suggest when Sonya would accept films blindly to please Ramola.

"It's your life, your career, your effort, your talent and your name… please value it, Di," Tania reprimanded her often.

Sonya often admired her younger sister's mature take on life and respected her opinion.

There were persistent knocks on her door. Sonya grunted knowing it was Ramola. She always knocked as if the house was on fire.

Ramola didn't wait for Sonya to answer, as she barged into the room, pushing her out of the way. She didn't care that Sonya was recovering from a traumatic experience.

"Sonya … the cop is here. I think this is regarding your accident that night."

Sonya stared at her aghast, wondering if Ramola had lost the last ounce of empathy.

"Should I send him away if you are not feeling up to it? I don't want you to end up creating more mess."

If this was Ramola's way of showing she cared, why not, thought Sonya.

"You don't have to. I can handle this," Sonya said grabbing her shawl.

Ramola offered to hold Sonya's hand, but Sonya waved her away.

Ramola never missed out on any opportunity to show the world how much she loved and cared for Sonya.

Despite resistance from Sonya, as she walked out to the living room, Ramola held her arm. Sonya let it be, as she did not want to create a scene.

The officer stood up and smiled as Sonya staggered to the couch.

Ramola called for the maid to get coffee and cookies for everyone.

"Sonya is still weak from all the medicines. I hope you keep this meeting to a minimum," Ramola spoke as if concerned. Inside, she was scared that Sonya would create a scene.

"Officer... I am fine. Mom, he is doing his job," Sonya dismissed her with a sharp look.

Ramola, miffed, sat on the nearby couch.

Sonya heard Tania's voice in her head. *"See, doing things your way does not harm you. Learn to say 'no'."*

That little voice in her head, gave her comfort. It was only when the darkness superseded Tania's voice that things turned ugly. Like the night of the accident. Sonya shuddered at the memory of losing control. Did she really lose control or...Sonya let the thought hang.

"Take command, Sonya... it's your life." Dr. Kulkarni had harped on this advice in every session.

Arjun's razor-sharp gaze had not missed the sparks that flew between the mother and daughter the moment they had walked in. The relationship lacked harmony, he noted.

Arjun turned to Sonya. She looked gorgeous even with a bare face. He could sense a tremendous amount of pain in her eyes, though. It was no surprise he was able to connect with Sonya's pain.

Arjun, with great difficulty, drew away his gaze and opened his notebook. The maid arriving with coffee served as a welcome distraction.

"I understand you are not too well, and I won't be taking much of your time," Arjun cleared his throat as Sonya glanced at him. Two seconds later, he realised she was staring at something past him. Strange, he thought, getting a bit perturbed.

"I hope no charges are levied on my daughter. No one was hurt in this accident," Ramola said curtly, obviously flustered by the way things were going.

Arjun was rudely drawn away from his thoughts. "Sonya Rana is responsible for rash and negligent driving. Her behaviour could be termed as dangerous for herself, and endangering others' lives."

Arjun was angry at the way Ramola was perceiving this matter and trying to brush away her daughter's fault. It was sheer audacity on her part to interfere in legal proceedings.

"Mom…" Sonya silenced her, followed by a steely gaze, and turned to Arjun. "I own up to my mistakes. I am ready to apologise in writing if that is needed. Do I need to pay a fine for any damage to public property? I am willing to do that. I will cooperate with you, officer." Sonya sounded weak but firm.

Arjun was taken aback by Sonya's compliance. He had expected tantrums and denials.

"I need you to come down to the police station and complete some formalities," Arjun threw a disconcerting look at Ramola, then to Sonya he said. "I can see you are still not up to it. I will work on this keeping in mind the legality of the issue."

"I understand what I did back there was ridiculous and irresponsible. I promise I won't repeat it, Officer," Sonya said with conviction.

Arjun got up to leave, telling her he would be in touch.

"Should I call for a lawyer, Mr. Deshmukh? Anything that needs to be done?" Ramola had bowed down before the law, noticed Arjun, her stance softened by now.

"It would be better if you send your lawyer over for the necessary paperwork," Arjun said as Gaurav walked him to the door.

"There was no need for you to apologise, Sonya. You are a star. Use your status. Didn't you see he was enamoured by your beauty?" Ramola rolled her eyes, obviously pleased by her observation. "Learn to use your charm, girl."

Sonya felt nausea building up within her. It was soon replaced by anger.

"Did you just pimp me to that officer? You treat me like an object with no feelings and emotions. Something you can use and throw," Sonya's voice had risen, unbeknown to her.

Ramola took a step back. She had not expected this kind of outburst from her daughter.

"I thought this woman here loved me, like a daughter. Someday, I hope, she will truly consider me her daughter, one day…"

"Stop yelling for no reason. Everybody is talking about your accident. Do you have any idea how it will reflect on your career? There is no dearth of new talent. If you continue to behave recklessly, very soon you will find yourself with no films," Ramola was furious as she lashed out at Sonya.

Sonya was breathing rapidly.

Say it, Mom, 'Daughter, you don't have to stress. Sometimes it's alright to let go.'

"That will be my last day alive." Sonya's tone was cold. Suddenly, something shifted inside her.

"I want to stop. Why don't you let me…? I am tired of all this," Sonya sobbed, and Tania chose to enter that very moment. "I am tired of living a lie."

"Mom… what's happening? Di… are you all-right?" Tania dropped the grocery bags and rushed to Sonya's side.

"Why do you keep pushing Di all the time? Let her be. If she does not want to work, why don't you just… give up? Get a life!" Tania was furious.

Tania glared at Ramola while Sonya stood trembling in her arms. She looked at the two girls standing in solidarity.

"I know what you two girls are up to," she threw a scathing look at Sonya.

"Let me tell you, Sonya. You are allowing your life to spiral. No one is responsible but you!" Ramola pointed a finger in her direction, hitting hard, driving her point home.

"I love you; I want you to hold me, assure me, love me…not hate me."

Sonya trembled with anger. Finally, she stormed into her room, banging the door shut. They could hear the click as the door locked.

Tania angrily marched towards her mother. There was so much she wanted to say, but there was this rage swelling inside her which made it difficult to speak.

Tania shook her head in disgust at her mom and ran towards her room, banging it shut. The sound of doors banging reverberated within the four walls.

Ramola stood there wondering what she had done. Gaurav excused himself and left.

$\mathcal{S}$even

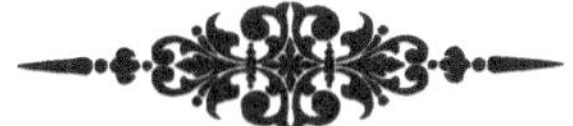

Arjun sat in the car, turning the conversation over and over in his mind. Something did not fit, he thought. Sonya had immediately accepted her mistake and apologised, but her mother… was she the problem? He was deep in thought, so he did not hear the car door open and somebody get in. A gentle nudge, and he jerked out of the trance he was in.

"Hello, Mr. Officer… you don't seem to be here?" Nandini gave a dazzling smile, her nose ring catching the early noon sunlight.

Arjun was surprised to see her. "You are a godsend. I am dying to speak to someone."

Nandini laughed, her brandy eyes shining. Arjun smiled as the soft curls bounced with every nod.

"Okay... shoot!" Nandini made herself comfortable next to him as they drove off. She loved to brainstorm with Arjun.

Nandini was a crime reporter with a news channel. She was young, bright, and resourceful. She was always one step ahead of her colleagues; hence, she climbed the ladder of success within no time of joining as a cub reporter.

"I met Sonya Rana today." Before he could say more, Nandini squealed excitedly.

"You met Sonya Rana... the Bollywood star... OMG! Why didn't you take me with you?" Nandini squeezed Arjun's arm in excitement, and he looked at her amused.

"Sorry..." Nandini let go but not before rattling off her craze for Sonya.

"Okay... stop... you want to hear me out?" Arjun rolled his eyes.

"Go on. I am all ears," Nandini said as she took out a packet of cookies and offered some to Arjun before munching on them.

"You need a sugar rush to brainstorm? Well, I don't mind," Arjun smiled, biting into the chocolate cookies as Nandini nodded her head.

Arjun wanted to smooth the stray locks that caressed her face, his gaze wandered to her lips. He ached to kiss the traces of chocolate from her lips. With great difficulty, Arjun turned his attention back to the road.

"I am waiting," Nandini said, oblivious to the effect she was having on Arjun.

Arjun cleared his throat, embarrassed, as if caught in his private rendezvous.

"What we witnessed the other night, Sonya's accident... it bothers me," Arjun stopped at the signal at a busy intersection. He turned to look at Nandini who had nearly finished the packet of cookies.

"The rate at which you eat those chocolate cookies!" He shook his head in utter disbelief. "I won't be surprised to see you running to a dietitian in the coming years."

Nandini glared at Arjun. "This is body-shaming."

Arjun was taken aback. "It's a suggestion which you will be thankful for in future."

Nandini grunted, changing the topic. "What aspect of the accident bothers you?" Nandini asked, wiping the remains of cookie crumbs off her face and hands. Arjun noticed the stubborn chocolate still stuck to her lips. He took Nandini by surprise when he wiped the bit of chocolate. His fingers lingered a bit longer than necessary. He noticed her blush.

"Oh... thanks." Embarrassed, she arched her eyebrow, turning away. His touch set butterflies fluttering in her stomach. A long silence ensued. They were caught in the afternoon traffic.

"Where were we…? Yeah… Sonya's accident! Was it intentional?", Arjun pondered on that for a moment before turning to Nandini.

"You mean suicide? I don't agree with you. Everyone knows her love for speed. She has driven sports cars before. I think it was an error of judgement. Maybe she was spooked by an oncoming car or blinded by the headlights. Dangerous and reckless is what best describes Sonya Rana!" Nandini saw it as an accident and nothing more than that.

"Hard to believe, but I think Sonya did it deliberately," Arjun was now confident about what he thought. "There was something dangerous on her mind… I am sure." He stopped the van outside a coffee shop.

Nandini let out a slow whistle. "It was a touch-and-go kind of madness… it could be just for the thrill! Indulgence of the reckless and the rich!"

Arjun loved the way her brandy eyes shone with excitement. He wondered if they turned smoky when aroused.

Arjun shook the wayward thoughts out of his mind, reminding himself he should be careful around her. Despite the reminder, he did something unimaginable.

"Thanks a lot for showing up. My treat…coffee?" he didn't wait for an answer and began walking towards the café. He wanted her to stay, spend some more time with her.

Later, as Nandini slurped on a chocolate milk shake and dug into chocolate-filled cookies, Arjun watched her with amusement.

"What?" Nandini looked up to find Arjun grinning.

"Nothing… your fascination with chocolate… just wondering where you put all that." His gaze travelled over her slim and petite frame.

Nandini chewed on her lower lip, smacking him on his head with the newspaper. Arjun liked the way she blushed; her cheeks dimpled.

Nandini wondered where this was leading. She had met Arjun one year ago during the double homicide involving mother-daughter. It had shocked the entire city. Nandini and Arjun were a team when it came to solving murder mysteries.

Nandini claimed she had the help of a mystic who could communicate with souls. Arjun refuted her belief, though he accepted the clues she provided on the case.

Nandini had finished her chocolate milk shake. She looked at her watch.

"Gosh, I am late! I forgot, I have a meeting scheduled with the editor. Got to leave." Nandini gathered her stuff, promising to meet again.

Arjun amused, looked at Nandini who hailed an auto. Arjun paid the bill and drove off, Nandini on his mind.

Eight

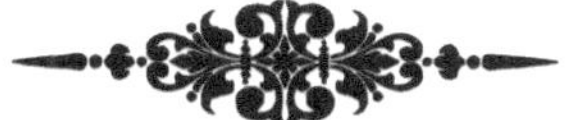

Sonya sat on the swing in her balcony, overlooking the city as it came to life. She looked up at the stars, the infinite blue sky, felt the breeze in the trees, and the scent of the sea mixing with elements of darkness. Suddenly, Sonya felt overwhelmed by it all and began sobbing.

"God why are you putting me through all this?" Sonya clutched her head. "My head is throbbing. God, please help me." Sonya put her head between her legs and sobbed. After a while, she got up, staggered over to the bedside table, and removed a bottle of Scotch.

Sonya carried the bottle to the swing and drank. She felt a little better, but the headaches continued. The bottle was nearly empty now, and Sonya let it roll on the floor. She realised alcohol had failed to calm the inner turmoil.

Sonya curled up on the swing and kept looking at the stars. She did not realise when she fell asleep. It was a disturbed sleep that took her into her childhood. It reminded her of the nightmare she had endured.

Sonya saw Vikram slowly walking towards her, making lewd gestures, saying her name, making her cringe.

"Sonya... Sonya... my little angel... come to your uncle."

Sonya was running through the corridors, glancing over her shoulder. She knew, within no time, Vikram would catch up and once again lay his dirty hands on her, soiling her body and her soul.

Sonya winced. She was now sitting on Vikram's lap, his hands moving over her back, groping her chest, caressing her cheeks, kissing her. Sonya, her eyes reflecting fear, pushed him away with her tiny arms.

"You like an angel... you like me touching you here..." His finger traced a path from her back to her tiny buttocks as he clasped them in his hands.

Sonya pushed him away, falling to the floor.

"Come here, you little witch. I am not going to let you go," Vikram ground his teeth, pulled Sonya by her hair, and roughed her up as the little girl winced in pain.

Sonya sobbed in her sleep, crying out in pain. She fought monsters from the past and willed the nightmares to go.

Tania, who dropped in to see how Sonya was doing, saw her crying in her sleep, her arms flailing. Tania placed Sonya's head in her lap and gently weaved her fingers through her hair, murmuring comforting words in her ears.

"Shh… shh… be quiet. You are safe. Vikram uncle will never come back." Tania rocked her in her arms like a mother would rock a baby.

Tania distinctly remembered that night when she had gone visiting Vikram uncle with her mother in New Jersey. It was snowing outside. Uncle offered a drink to her mom, while she sat drinking hot chocolate on a high stool in his kitchen.

"You did not bring Sonya along with you?" Vikram asked, his words slurring.

"Sonya is unwell. I came here to tell you that I am thinking of relocating to India. Now that Raghav is no more, I am unable to manage the business on my own," Ramola sighed.

"Don't go. What will you do in India?" Vikram said, alarmed. He was swaying under the influence of alcohol. Tania watched him stagger towards the couch where Ramola sat.

"*I am sending Tania away to boarding school,*" *Vikram turned to look at Tania, who appeared nonchalant to their conversation.*

"*What about Sonya? You can leave her with me. I will take good care of her. That way, you will have fewer responsibilities over your head… huh?*" *Vikram scratched his head, gulped down the drink and helped himself to another.*

Tania hated the lustful look on his face at the mention of Sonya Di.

"*I have plans for Sonya,*" *Ramola said with a determined look in her eyes.* "*Raghav never trusted you with Sonya. I discounted you because you were my brother.*" *Ramola stared hard at him.*

Vikram avoided meeting her gaze. He poured himself another drink.

"*You never considered her your daughter; why this fake empathy now?*" *Vikram smirked.*

"*Sonya is under my care. I am not going to hand her over to you. I knew you abused her…*" *Ramola whispered, glancing at Tania, making sure she was not listening.* "*I protected you because you are my brother,*" *Ramola got up, took hold of Tania, and walked out.*

Vikram called out to his sister, but Ramola ignored him, walking to the car. Tania looked back to see his face in the window, a scowl on his face. He was lighting a cigarette.

Tania smiled knowingly and waved. As they reached their car, they heard a loud explosion behind them. Ramola, shocked, turned to see flames rising from her brother's house. She dialled 911, shielding Tania from the horrific sight of the house burning down.

Tania brushed away her mother's hand. She saw her uncle's hand come up on the windowpane. His fingers, desperately clawing, calling for help. Ramola ran to the door, but Tania pulled her back, tears, and fear in her eyes. Ramola hugged her daughter, comforting her. By now, the flames had engulfed the main door too. Ramola stared in horror, watching her brother burn alive with the house.

Tania looked down at Sonya, who was still whimpering in her sleep.

"Shh ... shhh ... Vikram uncle will never ever trouble you, Di. I took care of him. Only if you could see how he suffered. He had to pay for hurting you,"

Tania gazed down fondly at her sister, who was still mumbling and shivering.

"You trust your sister, don't you? I am here... no one will dare hurt you," Tania patted Sonya's head. She had a faraway look in her eyes. The memories of that evening came flooding back again.

Ramola and Vikram were busy talking as little Tania sipped hot cocoa. She distinctly remembered a wave of anger arising in her whenever Vikram mentioned Sonya's name. Tania fiddled with the edge of her dress, her lips trembled, her eyes narrowed, and her breathing became hard. It had been so easy. Setting up a death trap for her uncle had been a cakewalk. She had unscrewed the gas pipe from the stove seconds before the two walked out of the house. She had often heard her dad warn their mother to be careful with the gas pipe and to switch off the mains once she shut the kitchen for the night. Tania had asked her father what would happen if the pipe had to come undone. Today, she had her answer.

Tania counted till ten as she saw Vikram clicking his lighter for a smoke.

"That was the end of Vikram ... the end of evil, Di." Tania smiled, but the next moment, a look of gloom passed over her face as she glanced at Sonya. Tania fondly kissed her forehead. Her eyes reflected possessiveness and determination to protect her sister from any harm whatsoever.

Tania gathered Sonya close to her bosom, giving her warmth, trying to ease her pain.

"Vikram is dead, but he left the seeds of evil in you. Finally, he got what he deserved." Tania lovingly patted Sonya's back.

"God, give me strength to protect Di against every evil." She prayed fervently.

Tears flowed freely from her eyes. Tania always was the stronger of the two. She never cried or showed her emotional side. It was only in solitude that she let the tears flow.

Tania kissed her sister on her forehead lovingly, rocking her in her arms. Tania hummed a song as she touched upon a fond memory from their childhood where the two sisters sat on the swing in the backyard of their house in New Jersey.

Nine

The girl in the black hoodie jogged around the pond in the park. Mist hung low, with sunrise hours away. A pair of wary eyes followed her every movement.

Tania noticed a young boy with a blue pea cap, pulled over his forehead, faded denims, those cheap ones you buy off the road, and a black t-shirt, faded and torn in many places. He was throwing suspicious glances at her, standing in shadows, she observed.

The black hoodie completed a circle and was now approaching in his direction. He let her pass by, waited, and then started jogging behind her, maintaining distance. He was familiar with the area, familiar with the regular users. This girl was new to him, hence extra caution. He had watched her look around, her eyes searching for someone as she jogged. He worked the area after all, late nights. He now took the lead, convinced, and nodded his head towards the rows of trees around the corner.

Tania followed the boy to one of the benches in the park. This was not her first time. She had been down this road before too. Tania walked over and sat down.

"How much do you need?" His voice was terse, and his eyes shifted nervously.

Tania rubbed her hands in nervousness. He glanced sideways at her.

"I hope you're not recording?" He shifted nervously, hands shaking, lips quivering.

Tania noticed sweat lining his forehead. Classic signs of a drug user, she noted.

"Of course not. I don't have time for such gimmicks," Tania threw back the hood and turned to him. It was important she gain his trust.

"I swear to God, I will cut you to pieces if you record this." The young boy was restless, tapping his feet, and chewing his nails.

"Shut up and show what you have. I don't have time for your bullshit." Tania muttered under her breath. The contact had told her this boy had what she needed.

"You have the dragonflies? I specifically want those." she muttered under her breath.

"I don't know what you are blabbering about. You got the wrong guy," he was still testing her, wary.

"You are in the wrong profession then. You wasted my time." Tania got up, dusting her shorts.

"Wait..." the boy said, bordering on faith and distrust. If he returned empty hand, his boss would beat him up.

"You must be kidding," Tania laughed, nodding her head. "I will speak to Abbas bhai about sending a novice."

"I will put in some extra from my side. Please don't rat me out to Abbas bhai," the boy looked around, now totally convinced this blue-eyed girl was serious about being a buyer.

Tania handed him a wad of five hundred rupee notes, and he gave her two packets of green capsules.

As soon as money and drugs were exchanged, both went in opposite directions.

Tania was sweating by now. She had done this before for herself, but this was the first time she was doing it for Sonya. After seeing Sonya suffering from tormenting dreams and alcohol abuse, she had thought, drawing from her own experience that drugs could act as a balm for Sonya's sufferings.

Tania was introduced to LSD by her roommate, Martha, who noticed Tania rarely slept, was always restless, and in a foul mood.

"A couple of pills and you will be fine," Martha said to her one night as Tania paced her room, flinging things around, raving and ranting.

Tania gave in to the temptation. "It worked," she squealed the next day. "Can she get some more?"

"It will cost you," said Martha.

It had indeed cost her a bit, but Tania worked double shifts to pay for drugs. She did not ask her mom for money as she knew the money her mom spent on her was from Sonya's earnings, and she did not want to cheat her sister of her hard-earned money.

Tania hid the stash in her jacket and broke into a slow jog, heading home. She had a solution for Di's troubles or at least she thought so.

Ten

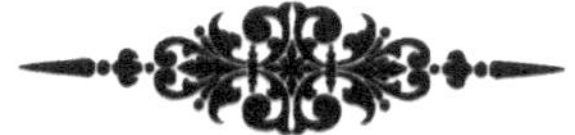

Two Weeks Later - Singapore

Sonya walked up to the bar in her suite, and to her dismay, it was empty. She cursed Ramola under her breath and instead poured herself a glass of water. She popped the pills Dr. Kulkarni had given her to take in case of an emergency. She refilled her glass and carried it to the window.

"Hmm ... mmm, waking up, getting out of the bed, feels like an ordeal." Sonya got under the blankets, slowly sipping on the water.

Sonya and her co-star Arnav were in Singapore for the last leg of the shoot. Some action scenes needed to be filmed this afternoon. She was booked into The Plaza in Marina Bay, in a suite. Keeping in mind her recent accident and fragile state of mind, Ramola and Gaurav had accompanied her to Singapore.

Sonya was in two minds about cancelling the shoot, but Ramola insisted she keep her commitments. Sonya gave it some thought. With Tania gone back to Canada and Jay busy with his job at his father's advertising firm, there was not much she could do back in India, so here she was, lazing in the bed, making the most of the shoot break.

The view from the 42nd floor was a total knock-out. The water in the Marina Bay shimmered in the afternoon sun. Everything seemed so minuscule. Sonya imagined she was a giant towering over tiny people and cars. Suddenly everything was at arm's length. She just had to reach out and pick up people and arrange them as per her whim. Sonya tried doing that but ended up knocking on the glass window. She giggled, finding it amusing.

Sonya staggered back, closed her eyes, shook her head, and once again looked at the scene below, her face to the window. The cars and the people still appeared close to her. What Sonya did not know was that she was hallucinating, experiencing side effects of the pills.

"Doc, your pills are magical! I am in control...I am in control." Sonya danced, bursting into laughter. Suddenly, a surge of sadness took over her and she broke down. She felt as if a metal claw clenched her heart and would rip it out any second. The room began to spin. Sonya was on the floor, gasping for breath. With great difficulty she sat up, taking in deep breaths.

"Think about the happy times…happy place. You can do this Sonya." Sonya reminded herself.

Once again, taking in a deep breath, Sonya closed her eyes and repeated to herself, "happy moments, happy moments", and then Tania's face flashed before her eyes. They were little girls once again, cycling towards the mountain path near their home in New Jersey. They reach an incline and Tania stops.

"Di, I am tired, can we rest for some time?" Tania points to her legs, telling her they hurt.

Soon, the cycles forgotten, the girls are chasing butterflies, running around the shrubs amidst tall trees, basking in the sunlight streaming through the tall trees, singing as they jump up and down, laughing, hand in hand.

Sonya hears Tania whisper in her ear and run away. As Sonya looks around, she sees lots of butterflies hovering above her. It seems hundreds of colours have exploded before her eyes. Suddenly she hears Tania calling out to her, "Sonya Di… Di… catch me, Di…"

A little while later, Ramola entered Sonya's suite with a duplicate key as Sonya did not respond to her knocks. On entering, she found Sonya on the floor, staring at the ceiling, non-responsive.

Ramola panicked and checked for a pulse and found one. Sonya's breathing was normal, but she was not responding to Ramola. Ramola started rubbing her palms, repeatedly calling out to Sonya, but she did not respond. Ramola helplessly looked around and dialled Gaurav's number.

Five minutes later, Gaurav was ringing the doorbell to Sonya's suite. He was shocked to see the state Sonya was in.

"Madam, I think we need to take her to the hospital. Sonyaji's condition…could get worse," Gaurav was loyal and sympathetic towards Sonya. When he was a newcomer, looking for work, Sonya had given him a chance and since that day he had not failed her.

"No … no hospital … you don't understand. If the word gets out…" Ramola was horrified at the thought. 'Imagine what will happen to Sonya's career.'

"Madam, Sonyaji's life is more important at this point…." Gaurav pleaded with her.

Ramola glared at him. "As if I don't care for her. You are forgetting she is my daughter."

"Sonyaji needs to be on set for the night shift." Sonya's condition further worried him. He was unsure if Sonya would make it to the shooting set today.

"Sonya will reach the set at the scheduled time, only if you help me now. Try to wake her while I speak to her doctor." Ramola snapped at Gaurav who splashed water on Sonya's face, gently patting her cheek.

Ramola rolled her eyes at him as she dialled Dr. Kulkarni.

"Mrs. Rana, can you get her to the hospital?"

"Doctor,…that is not the option." replied Ramola, curtly. "She has commitments here and think about her career. I am the one who will be left with a lot of answering to do. What should I tell the producer and the director?"

Ramola sounded very upset. She darted an angry look at Sonya who had stirred awake.

As she spoke to the doctor, Ramola checked the medicines and realised Sonya had overdosed on the emergency meds.

"Mrs. Rana, after this conversation, I have come to understand that Sonya is in your care. I still advise you to please take it slow with her. Sonya's mental condition is fragile."

"The emergency medicine that you prescribed…I have a feeling that Sonya overdosed on those." Ramola was shocked at this revelation.

For the doctor, Ramola came across as desperate. Dr. Kulkarni contemplated on Sonya's condition miles away.

"Judging from the condition you found her in... you must wake her up, give her water mixed with salt till she vomits. We will be able to dilute the side-effects to some level. Is it possible to understand how many pills she has had?"

Ramola sent Gaurav to get salt while she propped her up. Next, she checked the medicines and discovered that Sonya had taken six pills. She informed Dr. Kulkarni who told her it was not serious enough to cause harm to Sonya.

Gaurav returned promptly and under Ramola's instructions prepared the mixture. Ramola put the glass to Sonya's lips and coaxed her to drink. On second glass, Sonya puked.

Ramola applied cold compresses to an exhausted Sonya who slept the rest of the day. Ramola sat in a chair by her bedside, keeping close watch on her, alert.

Eleven

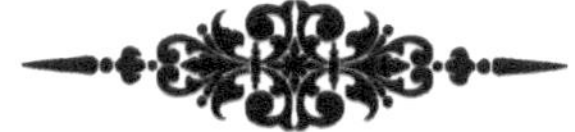

“*For I know the plans I have for you,*” *declares the LORD,* “*plans to prosper you and not to harm you, plans to give you hope and a future*”.

Tania, knelt in front of the statue of Mother Mary, head bowed. In her hands was a book of prayers. Tania was a frequent visitor to the Church in Toronto.

Tania had done her schooling from a convent boarding school. The nuns there found her to be agitated and anxious as a child. They tried counselling sessions for Tania. There was an old church on the campus, and one day Tania walked in the middle of a service. The priest let her attend the service, refraining from asking any questions to the seemingly disturbed girl. This continued for a week.

Tania realised she had found oneness with God when in church. It was here that she found peace and solace and hoped to find a way to help Sonya.

Tania was fiercely protective about Sonya, and even Ramola had no idea to what extent Tania could go.

Tania gazed deeply into the eyes of Mother Mary, whose huge statue stood in front of her holding her son, Jesus.

"Mother, I call upon you to protect my sister from evil, show her the way, may she find peace. Please help her, make her strong and keep her in your care."

Tania got up, looked forlornly at Mother Mary's kind face, and crossed her heart. She walked up to the pew and placed Sonya's picture in the healing box. Tania was desperate to put her faith in something that will provide her solace.

"From today onwards, I will be a mother to my sister. I will not let her hurt anymore." The blue in her eyes shone with determination as she lit a candle in the church.

Tania vowed she would do everything in this world for Sonya. She knew Ramola was not the best mother for Sonya or for her. She had been manipulative throughout the beginning, governed by selfish reasons.

"My mother failed in protecting her daughter, so now, it is up to me to protect my sister." Tania became her sister's self-proclaimed protector from the day she had come upon Vikram's monstrous act towards Sonya. Something within had snapped that day, and Tania was no longer the innocent child she was then! Ramola failed to understand the emotional turmoil Tania was going through.

It was her love for her sister that drove her to kill Vikram that day. She had sensed no fear, no remorse since, but her sister was miles away from peace. Vikram's shadow still haunted Sonya, and their mother's indifference was painful.

Tania cared. Sonya was her family and don't we defend our family from evil! She reasoned with herself.

Twelve

Singapore looked beautiful and alluring, bathed in evening lights. The poolside of the hotel was busy as the director finished canning a shot and announced pack-up for the night.

Ramola had arrived on the sets to escort Sonya to her room. She was not taking any chances now, away from home. Gaurav saw Ramola and hurried over to her.

'"Sonyaji gave a brilliant shot. Director Mohan Sir is so happy that he wants to sign Sonyaji for his next movie," Gaurav said excitedly.'

"I hope Sonya's state of mind continues to remain the same." Thinking about that afternoon sent a shiver down her spine.

Sonya regained consciousness after four hours. She was not able to make it to the sets on time. Ramola requested Sujoy to adjust the shoot timings as Sonya was slightly unwell. When Mohan heard this, he decided he would shoot the scenes first, where Sonya was not required. Ramola had personally thanked them and breathed a sigh of relief. She hoped and prayed that the next few days pass uneventfully.

"Gaurav, I hope you are sending out fillers to the press and share her pictures with the PR team," Ramola gave all these instructions keeping a watchful eye on Sonya who was by the pool, laughing with Arnav.

Then, Ramola noticed something. Mohan was sitting a few metres away and was continuously staring at Sonya. His gaze travelled all over Sonya as he followed her every movement. "This man is crazy for Sonya," observed Ramola. "This is a good sign," Ramola said to herself.

Gaurav broke into her thoughts. "Madam, should I post the news about Sonyaji doing a life-threatening stunt for this movie?" Hearing this, Ramola's heart skipped a beat.

"What are you saying? What stunt? Is she out of her mind?" Gaurav was surprised as he had not expected Ramola's reaction. He believed Ramola cared less about what Sonya did.

Sonya burst into giggles as Arnav cracked a joke, when Ramola walked over and swung her by her arm to face her.

"Mom, what's wrong with you?" Sonya appeared flustered, wincing at the pain where Ramola had grasped, leaving angry red marks.

"What am I hearing? You are planning to do a life-threatening stunt? Is that true?" Ramola trembled, hoping Sonya would deny it as a rumour.

That evening, the production team had discussed the scene requiring Sonya to leap from a high rise. Sujoy had arranged for a body double for the stunt, and Mohan seconded his suggestion. Sonya put her foot down. She had decided she would do this stunt herself.

Sujoy and Mohan knew how stubborn Sonya could be. Now it was a task to assure Ramola that all safety measures would be in place. Before they could have a word with her, she had heard it from Gaurav.

"Mom, please, stay out of this. I know I can do this, and I want to." Sonya freed her arm from Ramola's grip and walked away.

Ramola stood there, looking at her daughter's retreating back, shocked.

"I tried to dissuade her, but you know your daughter well," Sujoy had witnessed the heated exchange between mother and daughter. "I have a body double on standby if Sonya changes her mind."

Sujoy's words were reassuring, but Ramola knew Sonya would never change her mind.

Later, Ramola angrily paced the room, while Sonya calmly sipped on a special mocktail as Ramola guarded her with a gaze of a hawk. After that incident, Ramola made sure there was no alcohol in her suite.

"Are you out of your mind? You want to jump from a high-rise and want me to take it cool?" Ramola shouted, obviously angry at the preposterous decision that Sonya had taken, that too without consulting her.

If Sonya was perturbed by all the ranting and shouting by Ramola, she did not show it.

"It's how you view it. I perceive it as a Leap of Faith," Sonya said calmly. She had walked up to Ramola, giving her a challenging look. Ramola stared dumbfounded at her.

"Mom… you want me to remain on top, don't you?" Ramola noticed a trace of madness in Sonya's eyes. Her words were not hers. Ramola, for a moment, felt she was speaking to a stranger with enough coldness to freeze a person's heart.

"I will be on top of this world once I complete this stunt… mark my words!" Sonya smiled, setting a mocking tone.

"I shall go down in the history of Bollywood to be the first actress to perform such a dangerous stunt." Sonya was breathing rapidly; her cheeks were flushed.

As Ramola looked at her with disbelief, Sonya continued to stare ahead for a while then as if nothing had happened, reached out for the earphones and curled up on the recliner. Ramola had very few options but to leave the room.

Sonya's personality had undergone a major shift since they had come to Singapore, noted Ramola. This new Sonya was impossible to manage.

Thirteen

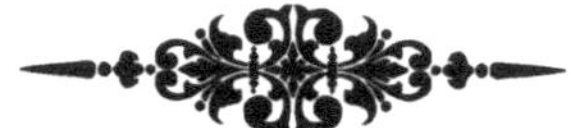

Sonya took a deep breath. She could feel the adrenaline pumping through her veins. The wind howled, swaying her gently. Next to her stood Arnav, tense. There was a helicopter hovering a little distance away, ready for an aerial shot. Around her, hundreds of people shouted instructions to each other. The atmosphere was electric and tense. Sujoy stood to their right, looking up at them.

"Sonya… Arnav, you can still change your mind," his lips pursed, "I have body doubles waiting."

Arnav was not enthusiastic about doing the stunt himself, but when Sonya refused a body double, and he was left with very little choice. His male ego clashed with his fear and reasoning.

Ramola, worried, looked at what her daughter was up to from a few feet away. "Sonya is suicidal, but what about Arnav? Has he too left his brains at home?" She was frustrated as Sonya had defied her.

"If Arnav sir had stood his ground yesterday and convinced her otherwise, I think Soniya ji would have considered using a body double," Gaurav spoke softly, careful not to be overheard.

"Men and their inflated egos," Ramola sat down on the chair from where the monitor was visible. She could hear Sonya's incessant chatter and laughter.

"Don't worry, Sujoy. I am loving this. You too should try doing this… take a leap of faith! What say, Arnav?"

Arnav nodded grimly, hoping Sonya was right. Sonya winked, took a deep breath, and steadied her body, like a yogi.

"Leap of faith, my head. I hope Sonya knows what she is talking about," Ramola mumbled.

Sujoy had seen a strange determination flash in Sonya's eyes that afternoon, and it scared the hell out of him.

Cameras were poised, pin-drop silence on the floor as the director waited for a signal from the cinematographer. People chewed nails in anticipation, hearts beating and excitement palpable in the air. Sujoy and Mohan watched from behind the monitor with bated breath.

Sonya kept her eyes open. She wanted to experience and sense the fear as she jumped. Was this fear more than the darkness that gripped her heart, the cold that froze her mind, or the evil that ravaged her brain cells? Sonya glanced up at the infinite sky above and then at the world below. If you jump down, you go up! Now that was just so conflicting. Death was a dilemma she had dwelt on for long now. Today, if she died, she would have no qualms as it would be her destiny, like the other day when she had driven Jay's car over the ledge. She had come away unscathed. It was time to find out.

Sonya heard Mohan say 'action' as the wind howled around her. Sonya, without giving much thought, jumped, and so did Arnav. She was screaming as she went down, clutching to the safety harness.. They were instructed not to flail their arms for the jump to appear professional. The walls, the buildings around her zoomed in supersonic speed, windows blurred into one, a splash of colours attacked her vision, blood curdled within, and her scream sounded alien to her until she could no longer hear her own scream. Cameras from all four sides captured their jump beautifully.

Within five minutes, it was over. The scene was canned as per the action director's instructions. A few minutes later, a jubilant Sonya and Arnav walked in, cheek flushed, breathing laboured, wide grin. The assistant directors picked Sonya up and paraded her like a trophy. She was the first female actor to do such a daring stunt without a body double. Arnav slumped down on the chair, not believing he was still alive and breathing!

Sonya glanced over at Ramola, who had shock and fear written on her face.

"I am alive and well, Mom," Sonya gave her a jubilant smile.

Ramola stood there speechless. She knew this madness was not going to stop here. This was just the beginning!

Fourteen

The Rolling Stone Pub in 'The Plaza' was where the action was this evening! People took to the dance floor like crazy. The film crew had worked hard the entire day and were now letting their hair down. Sonya sat aloof from all this madness in one corner, nursing her drink.

Mohan entered the pub and went over to where Sujoy sat with other crew members. His eyes eagerly searched for someone, and then he saw what he was looking for. He saw Sonya, lost in herself, drunk, sitting in one corner.

Sonya did not want to come here tonight, but Sujoy insisted, and now here she was! Through her glazed eyes, she saw Mohan approaching towards her. Sonya was not planning to have company. After the stunt, Sonya felt lightheaded. She had started liking this feeling! Sonya realised she should include more adventure and dare in her life to get that high!

"Hello, Sonya…" Mohan was already seated before Sonya could say anything, and that unsettled her a bit.

Mohan was young and handsome. He was a Casanova flitting among girls. For a long time, he had wanted to get close to Sonya. Today, he thought it was a wonderful opportunity. Sonya was away from home, lonely, drunk, and sad.

"Congratulations! Cheers on that daring feat you achieved today," Mohan touched his glass to hers as Sonya gave him a wary look. "It was a brilliant performance, and I am impressed." Mohan waited for Sonya's reaction but got only a wry smile in return.

"Mohan, if it's not too much to ask, I want to be left alone," Sonya said, crossing her long legs, unmindful of the hem of the dress exposing her thighs.

Mohan found her every movement tantalising. But Sonya was ignoring him, and he was offended.

Her phone rang. It was Jay. Sonya glared at Mohan who stepped away, giving her privacy.

"Hey, babes! What crazy stunts are you up to?" There was worry in his tone.

Sonya could not hear over the loud noise in the pub, so she stepped out.

"Baby... don't worry... I am good. I did well, huh!" Sonya chirped happily.

"Jay, if you had been here, I am sure you would have been proud," Sonya was now pacing back and forth in the lobby outside the pub, excited about the dangerous stunt she had pulled off.

"Take it slow, babes. After what you went through recently... I don't want you taking such risks. I am surprised Ramola let this happen," Jay expressed his concern for Sonya's safety.

"I can join you in Singapore. We can spend some quiet time... just the two of us," he crooned long distance, and Sonya hummed, loving the feel of his voice.

"I miss you. I will be home soon, Jay."

Sonya did not realise Mohan was standing behind her. It was only when she said her goodbyes to Jay and turned that she nearly collided with him.

He pulled her close, his face inches away from Sonya's.

"What are you doing? Let me go," Sonya squirmed, trying to loosen his grip, but he was strong.

"Hey darling... come, let's go," Mohan started dragging Sonya to a secluded spot. her.

Suddenly, Sonya was once again that little girl in her New Jersey home, sitting on Vikram uncle's lap. Vikram was staring at her with lust, his hands caressing her, and his tongue flicking in and out of her mouth. She heard voices, alarmed, coaxing her to run, hide. Sonya pushed Vikram away and saw it was Tania who was waving her hands frantically, urging her to come to her, holding the door open for Sonya.

"Di … run Di … hide … he is a monster, Di." Little Tania was calling out to her, urging her to follow her to a safe place.

Sonya came to her senses and was shocked to find herself in the hotel elevator. Mohan must have dragged her there when she was too stunned to react.

Mohan began kissing Sonya, his hands travelling all over her. She could feel his hand pushing up her dress. His touch felt cold and dirty. Sonya was filled with disgust. She pushed hard at Mohan, who was taken by surprise. She stabbed his foot with the heel of her stilettos. Mohan screamed in pain, stumbled, and banged his head on the number panel. Sonya desperately pressed her floor number and kept pressing, one eye on Mohan who was still on the floor, writhing in pain. Finally, after what seemed to be harrowing minutes, the elevator stopped on the 42nd floor, and Sonya staggered out, dazed. She could see Mohan struggling to get up. She ran without looking back and entered her room, locking it behind her.

✳ ✳ ✳

Sonya stood under the shower, fully clothed for a long while. She sobbed, hugging herself.

"Why did this have to happen to me? Why…what have I done? I don't deserve this." She screamed.

Sonya rubbed herself furiously until her skin turned red. She could still feel Mohan's hands on her. She desperately wanted to remove every trace of him.

Sonya now sat on the bed; towel wrapped around herself. She reached for her handbag and started rummaging for the pills. Sonya panicked and looked around for meds prescribed by Dr. Kulkarni, something to calm her down. Thankfully, she found the sedatives. Sonya took an extra dose, gulping them down with water. She curled into a cocoon, hugging her body tightly. Slowly she drifted into a medicated sleep. She had forgotten the count of days she had fallen asleep naturally or dozed off. The last thought was that of Mohan dragging her into the lift. Vikram too invaded her dreams, in between. Her sordid past was like a can of worms. Once opened, it chewed her insides.

Sonya was awakened by loud knocking sounds. She sat up, the towel still wrapped around her body.

The knocking continued, louder.

"Sonya … open the door," For a moment, Sonya thought she was back home in Mumbai. Then she looked at her wrists and thighs and noticed the bruises, and the last night's images flashed, making her nauseous. She rushed to the bathroom and puked. Sonya splashed water on her face and stared at her face. Her eyes were puffy from all the crying.

When Sonya opened the door, Ramola had begun to worry. She appeared to be anxious and agitated.

"There you are. What took you so long?" Ramola then looked at the towel-clad Sonya, surprised. "You are up and bathed so early? That's new to me. And here I thought, I had to wake you up."

Ramola didn't notice the distressed expressions on Sonya's face. Sonya followed Ramola around the room, wanting to say something, but she couldn't put the words together. Oblivious to Sonya's turmoil, Ramola switched on the kettle.

"Let me make you some tea. You will feel fresh." Ramola talked about the shoot and the costume trial, ignoring Sonya.

"Mom…mom…listen to me…" Sonya began to pluck her hair and chew her nails as a tremor rushed through her body. She clutched her head tightly and screamed. Ramola was shocked.

"I am going back. I can't do this," Sonya sat on the bed, her feet tapping, looking around nervously.

"Are you crazy? They are waiting to shoot with you and you…" Ramola looked at Sonya closely and then saw the bruises around her wrists, on her neck.

"What happened?" Ramola held her wrists. "Did you try to hurt yourself?" Ramola asked, shocked.

Sonya furiously nodded her head, tears streaming down her face. "No … no … It was not me."

"Someone did this to you? Who hurt you?" Sonya could feel a tremble in Ramola's voice.

Sonya was so overwhelmed that she broke down crying, her hands going around Ramola's waist, not letting go. For a second the thought her mom cared was overwhelming and comforting.

"Sonya … tell me, what happened?" Ramola coaxed her into confiding. Never had she done this mother-daughter thing, as far as Sonya was concerned, but today she knew she had to be empathetic towards Sonya. A lot of things depended on how Sonya reacted and behaved. Ramola did not want to aggravate her mental condition any further. Not with Dr. Kulkarni thousands of miles away.

Sonya was getting hysterical, sobbing intermittently, then going quiet, and then once again bursting into tears. Ramola offered her a glass of water, which she drank thankfully.

Sonya now slept in Ramola's lap. Her body shook with spasms; tears trickled down her face. Sonya had narrated exactly what had taken place with her. It seemed like déjà vu for Ramola.

That evening was etched in her mind, a memory so strong it refused to fade, and Ramola still despised Sonya for that.

Ramola was busy attending to little Tania. Sonya was sitting nearby, colouring. The doorbell rang, and Sonya ran towards the door. On seeing Vikram, she stepped back, but nevertheless, Vikram picked her up and carried her to the living room.

Sonya was an early bloomer. She was eight but she looked like an eleven-year-old. Vikram set her down on his lap and offered her chocolates. Sonya seemed uncomfortable, wriggling to get off, but Vikram held her firmly by her shoulders.

"Why do you bring chocolates for Sonya every day? Don't pamper her too much," Ramola expressed her displeasure. She did not like her brother lavishing attention on Sonya.

"I like bringing chocolates for her. She is my niece too, just like Tania, and I am fond of her."

Vikram said, kissing Sonya on her cheek. At that moment, Raghav entered, and Ramola saw him frown.

"Sonya, go to your room right now," Raghav's eyes were filled with rage. Sonya immediately made good of the opportunity and ran to her room. He threw a scathing look in Vikram's direction and walked away without a word.

Later, after Vikram had left, Raghav called Ramola and sat her down.

"I know you despise Sonya," Ramola tried to defend herself, but Raghav shushed her with a wave of his hand. "Sonya is a child and needs a mother. That's the reason I married you, but you don't seem to care."

"This is not fair, Raghav, after all that I do for you and our family… to keep our family together," Ramola could feel anger boiling inside her.

"Have you observed Sonya in the last few days? She seems disturbed, especially around your brother," Raghav grimly looked at Ramola, who furrowed her eyebrows as if trying to recollect.

"That's what I mean by saying that you are not paying enough attention to Sonya. She is growing up and she needs you. I won't be here forever, Ramola. I want you to be her mother, to take Meher's place," Raghav had a faraway look in his eyes.

"Raghav ... I love Sonya as much as you do. I reprimanded Vikram today about pampering Sonya. I will take care of that, don't worry," Ramola gave him an assuring smile, but Raghav still seemed disturbed.

"What is it that's bothering you?" Ramola began kneading his shoulder, trying to relax him.

"I don't like Vikram's proximity to Sonya. The other day she said he tried to kiss her. How long has this been happening?" Raghav said, discomfort evident in his voice.

"Listen, Ramola, Vikram is your brother; you should talk to him. This behaviour is inappropriate. Don't force me to take harsh steps."

Raghav got up and left as Ramola sat fuming. She was furious at Sonya for spreading lies about her brother.

Ramola marched upstairs to Sonya's room. Sonya was reading a book in her bed when Ramola stormed in angrily, closing the door behind her.

"What have you gained by telling lies about my brother to your father? Answer me," Ramola's eyes were filled with anger.

"Mom... I... Vikram, uncle..." Sonya stammered at the sudden onslaught. Ramola took hold of her arm and hauled her roughly out of the bed.

"You love this house, this family, don't you? You love your dad?" Sonya nodded her head in fear.

"You love your little sister, don't you?" Ramola shook her until Sonya's teeth rattled and her hair flew over her face.

"Yes, mom, I love you all, I promise..." Sonya now sobbed, helpless at her stepmother's ire.

"Then you don't want to go away from your family, do you?" Ramola's tone was threatening. Sonya shook her head.

"If you utter one more word against Vikram, I swear to God I will send you away so far from here, that you won't be seeing any of us for a long, long time. Do you get it?"

"Yes, mom, I understand," Sonya said, her eyes wide with terror, her voice trembling. She did not want to be lonely. She wanted to be close to her father and her little sister. It was a big price to pay for her family, but she would do it," thought Sonya.

Ramola hated being in the bad books with her husband. Raghav trusted her blindly, and the very foundation of their relationship was being threatened by Sonya. How could she possibly allow it!

Fifteen

Mohan sat in the chair, nursing his wounds, furious. He had nearly finished the Scotch. Sujoy snatched the bottle from him.

"What the hell were you thinking? You misbehaved with Sonya? …you…" Sujoy was afraid of the outcome of it all. He knew Sonya very well. She was professional, a no-nonsense girl who kept to herself, didn't socialize and was a dream to work with. Then Ramola's face flashed before his eyes, and suddenly he began to feel a headache building. He glared at Mohan.

"You know the amount of money riding on this project. I didn't expect this kind of behaviour from you." Sujoy was furious as he paced. This was his second movie as a producer, and he had high hopes. It was his dream to work with Sonya who was talented and was rumoured to bring success to any project she was a part of.

Suyog's phone rang. It was Gaurav.

"Oh ... wow! Time to face the music!" Sujoy wrung his hands in frustration.

Seconds later, they heard loud, angry knocks on the door and the bell kept buzzing. Sujoy opened the door to a furious Ramola, followed by Sonya and Gaurav, who stormed in.

Sonya looked at Mohan and marched towards him. She pulled him by his collar and slapped him hard across his cheek. Her body trembled, eyes swollen, hair askew.

Mohan staggered back and fell, twisting his ankle. He shielded himself from Sonya's blows. Sonya continued to kick him until Sujoy and Gaurav intervened.

"Sonya... listen to me... calm down. I am taking care of all this," Sujoy inserted himself between Sonya and Mohan.

"I am going to the police. The hotel's CCTV must have a recording of what happened last night. I will see to it that he rots in hell," Sonya said angrily.

Ramola had not seen Sonya lose her temper like this and was afraid of what was to follow.

Sonya seethed with fury. No longer did she feel helpless. Mohan had awakened the sleeping demons from the deep recesses of her mind. Last night she had dreamt of Vikram abusing her as a child. Once again, she had relived the horror of his touch, felt his lust consume her soul, and this time there was no hiding place or Tania to protect her. She was falling into a deep abyss.

Ramola gently held Sonya back and hugged her to calm her down. Ramola knew this issue had to be resolved within the four walls. She had to sweet-talk Sonya into letting go of what had transpired between her and Mohan last night, for the moment at least.

"Sonya… Sonya, listen to me, child. Look at me… here. I am your mother, you will listen to me, baby?" Ramola sat her down in the adjacent room, gave her some prescribed pills, insisting Sonya have them. Ramola patted her hand and lovingly smoothed her hair.

"Mom, what Mohan did last night…" she let her voice trail and sobbed. "It's unforgivable."

"Of course, what he did was very wrong and uncalled for," she chose her words carefully. "You did right by beating him up and showing him his place. Any other girl in your place would have reacted the same way as you did." Ramola's tone was cajoling and comforting.

Sonya was surprised to hear her mom supporting her, but she liked it, nevertheless.

"Why don't you rest for a while in your room and leave it to me. You trust me, right?" Ramola asked, making her concern sound as genuine as possible.

Ramola knew she had to resolve this matter amicably. There was a lot of money riding on this. Sujoy had made the payment upfront. The money was safely deposited in Ramola's bank account, unknown to Sonya. If Sonya did not deliver, she would have to return the signing amount.

Gaurav accompanied Sonya to her room. Ramola went back to where Mohan and Sujoy waited impatiently.

"Ma'am, Sonya was giving me hints… I thought Sonya also wanted… I mean…" Mohan was rudely cut off here by Ramola, who was looking at him pointedly.

"Sujoy, I will convince Sonya to stay back and complete the shoot on one condition. I want you to fire this guy right away. He should not be seen on the sets. Get a new director on board or else I am going straight to the Indian embassy," Ramola thundered.

"Where will I get a new director from at this hour? This is the last schedule of my film," Sujoy sounded helpless.

"I am trying to save his ass here and yours too," Ramola pointed at Mohan and gave Sujoy a scathing look. "You know Sonya very well. She will follow through her threat."

Sujoy contemplated Ramola's offer. After a long pause, he nodded his head, indicating he agreed with what Ramola had to say.

"It's best for everyone that you leave. My assistant will drop you to the airport," Sujoy called his assistant and briefed him.

Mohan, reluctant, left the room, murmuring in displeasure, threatening under his breath.

"Ramola ma'am, I hope you will manage Sonya. As of now, the chief assistant director will take over from here. I hope this incident stays between us." Sujoy worried about his movie and did not want the shoot disrupted.

"Thanks. I will handle Sonya. She will report to the sets as planned," said a confident Ramola as Sujoy, worried, looked on.

Sonya's reputation was at stake. The incident could well be turned to work in Sonya's favour. Someone had aptly put it, "Bad publicity is good publicity." Ramola grinned; satisfied things were working in her favour.

Sixteen

"**M**om, mom…" Jay waltzed in through the door, checking every room, excited, bursting with news.

Sandhya kept aside the book she was reading and walked to open the door when Jay pushed the door and entered. He held her arms and swung her around.

"Jay, be careful…what has got into you today?" Sandhya took in the happiness reflected on Jay's face. He had always been like this; a happy-go-lucky kid, brimming with optimism.

"Your son has bagged a huge client today, and that too, after a month of joining dad's ad agency," Jay clapped for himself.

"I am proud of you. Come here…" Sandhya pulled him in a hug. At that moment, Rishabh entered.

"What about this poor husband of yours who slogs day and night? Not a word of appreciation!" Rishabh feigned anger.

"Dad, please, you are stealing my moment here," Jay playfully complained as Sandhya agreed with her son.

"Let our child bask in the glory of his success." Sandhya said darting a proud look at Jay.

As Jay stepped away to check his phone, Rishabh apprised his wife about Jay's brilliant strategy that led them to bag such an important client.

Jay had received a notification on WhatsApp. One of his friends had sent a link to a video. Noticing Sonya's picture on the link, he opened it. The video was that of Sonya and Mohan in the elevator. Though it was not clear, he could see that Mohan had his arms wrapped around Sonya and they were kissing. Jay nearly dropped the phone. For a moment, he went numb, not knowing how to react. Then anger took over.

"How could you do this, Sonya..." he kept muttering to himself, disbelief evident in his voice.

Moments later, Sandhya heard Jay fuming, followed by the front door banging shut. She was at the door when she heard the elevator doors open.

"Jay ... Jay ... what happened? Rishabh ... why did Jay leave abruptly? What's wrong?" Sandhya went to the balcony and saw Jay driving away as Rishabh looked clueless.

"What's wrong with him? One moment he was happy and suddenly he rushed out. Try calling him." Rishabh was worried.

"He behaves like this when he gets a call from Sonya" Sandhya murmured.

Sandhya was aware of Sonya's fragile state of mind. In the past, there were many instances when Jay had to leave in the middle of the night when Tania would call from Canada, saying that Sonya was unwell, or she was not answering calls and Jay should go check on her. Now, Sandhya hoped the girl was fine. Her calls to Jay went unanswered.

Jay increased the volume and hoped for the beat of the music to take over the thoughts that raced through his mind. What had driven Sonya to do this? Why? What was the need? Or was Sonya forced to do it? The questions haunted him.

Jay screeched to a halt and dialled Sonya's number. It rang for a while and then disconnected on its own. Jay was about to give up when his cell rang. It was Rohit, his best friend since school.

"Hey Jay, I went over to your house. Where are you? Aunty sounded worried."

"Rohit, meet me at the cafe on Juhu Circle. I want to talk to you. It's important." A nagging thought about Sonya disturbed Jay.

Rohit reached the café in ten minutes. He could see Jay was already seated by the window.

"Hi… what are you doing here? Aren't you supposed to be in a client meeting?" Rohit was clueless at the helplessness his friend was feeling.

Rohit dreamt of becoming an actor. He would give auditions and if luck was on his side, bag a small role in series or films. Jay helped him by putting in a word with his contacts in advertising or wherever he could. He had spoken to Sonya, and she had readily agreed to help Rohit.

Jay weaved his hands through his thick dark hair and clutched his forehead tightly.

"Jay, are you okay, buddy? What's wrong, man?" Rohit asked, getting alarmed. "Is Sonya okay?"

"Something is not right, Rohit. I can sense it," Jay said, mulling over the thought in his mind.

"It's Sonya… isn't it?" Rohit asked, looking at Jay, urging him to say something.

Rohit knew that Jay and Sonya were best friends, and Jay always worried about the latter. Sonya's state of mind was fragile. Jay had to be very careful around Sonya. It was like walking on eggshells. He was in love with Sonya and when he tried to express his feelings, Sonya would distance herself from Jay. Her behaviour was confusing and not easy to comprehend.

"This afternoon I received a video of Sonya and Mohan, the director of the film she is working in. They were… Rohit, I can't even…" Jay had tears in his eyes. Rohit's heart went out for his friend. Being with Sonya needed every ounce of energy.

"That video could be just a publicity stunt. You never know," Rohit hoped to comfort his friend.

Jay wanted to believe Rohit's theory. It could be possible. Nowadays, linking co-actors was part of a publicity stunt.

"Why didn't Sonya tell me any of this? Last evening, we were on call," Jay's voice evoked disbelief. He expected Sonya to deny the entire thing. She must be aware of this video making rounds in the media. Soon it will hit television channels and give rise to a new controversy.

"Holy smokes!" Rohit exclaimed, looking out of the window. Jay followed his gaze.

"If thoughts had wings," mumbled Jay.

Press vans were lining up outside the coffee shop. Cameramen and photographers made a beeline for the door. Some of them had spotted Jay at the window, cameras focused on him, patrons watched, flummoxed.

"We need to get out of here, Jay." Rohit pulled him by his sleeve and headed for the back door. They had outsmarted the press or so they thought, when he saw a couple of them had positioned themselves outside the rear exit, waiting for Jay to make an appearance. They had no choice but to step out.

"Jay, what do you think about the video of Sonya and Mohan Kashyap?"

"Is it for real?"

"Do you think it's a publicity stunt ahead of the release?"

The questions were coming fast, and Jay panicked.

Rohit took the car keys from Jay and got away from the melee, leaving Jay to handle the press on his own for a while. The plan was, Rohit would get the car ready so that they could make good their escape.

Jay mumbled, "No comment." for every question and started making his way through the crowd. From the corner of his eye, he saw his car parked a few metres away, Rohit at the wheels.

The press people had surrounded him, and when it seemed almost impossible to escape, he halted. They were taken by surprise. He was going to say something, they thought, happily.

Jay had assessed the situation and knew he had to give them something.

"I have faith in Sonya. It is better we wait for her to get back and give statement," Jay was about to make a run for the car when a question from a journalist froze him.

"Mohan Kashyap tried to assault Sonya in Singapore during the shoot of their film. Is this true?"

All eyes turned to Nandini, and suddenly frantic calls were being made, each one trying to confirm the news. Nandini made her way towards Jay.

"What did you say? Sonya was assaulted? Oh… oh." Jay was shaken as he tried to make sense of this news. Suddenly, an immense sense of guilt took over. Why hadn't he thought of this? Why did he assume that Sonya was playing along?

Rohit had brought the car around and was frantically signalling him to get in. Nandini waited for Jay to answer.

Jay appeared devastated as he said, "No comment," and got into the car. He shut his eyes and leaned back.

"Sonya, I am so sorry, I wasn't there to protect you." He sobbed as Rohit drove in silence.

Seventeen

Sonya was back in Dr. Kulkarni's consulting room. She was pacing, restless and agitated. This time around it was Jay who waited outside for her as Tania was in Canada. Dr. Kulkarni played the role of observer, patiently waiting for Sonya to settle down.

Ramola had briefed him about the incident that had transpired at the hotel in Singapore. The sexual assault further nailed the depression. Dr. Kulkarni was confident that driving the car over the ledge, overdosing and now the life-threatening stunt was a cry for help.

In twenty years of being a psychiatrist, the doctor had come across patients struggling with various forms of mental health issues. In cases of severe depression, the patient always harboured thoughts of ending their own life. And Sonya had many a time stated her wish to die.

One look at Sonya and the doctor knew that she was dangerously close to the edge of the precipice. Sonya was not being honest with him, and hence, his hands were tied. There was definitely some kind of trauma she had experienced in her childhood that had manifested and defined her adulthood. Sonya was already facing abandonment issues because of her birth mother, but there was something else that sent the girl spiralling into a deep, dark place. Dr. Kulkarni genuinely wanted to help the girl. At this moment, he felt helpless. Ramola had also maintained a stoic silence on her part. Time was running out for her.

Suddenly, Sonya sat down on the couch and picked up the coloured pencils. Her actions were frenzied. Doctor Kulkarni noted down his observations. Not a word had been exchanged in the past fifteen minutes into the session. After five minutes or so, Sonya stopped sketching, looked up, and turned the sketch towards the doctor.

Dr. Kulkarni was aghast at the sketch Sonya had put together. When he looked at her, Sonya's eyes were filled with tears. She was tugging at her hair, lips quivering. A slight tremor passed through her. Dr. Kulkarni removed his glasses and leaned back, shocked.

Eighteen

The room was unkempt and bereft of any furniture. A futon was thrown on the floor, and a small television set took up one corner. Half-empty food containers lay nearby. The open kitchen was a mess, with the sink full of cups and plates. The door opened, and a woman who had seen better days walked in. She threw the keys on the table by the door and slumped into the futon. She was carrying mail which, to her disdain, were mostly bills. She was looking for something, which was evident in the way she flung the envelopes on the floor and lit a cigarette. She lay on the futon, staring at the ceiling, which was lined with cobwebs and cracks running through and through. Her eyes became moist as her brain touched upon a memory from the past.

Meher was in her twenties when she was married off by her parents to Raghav, who was an NRI. Meher's dream of pursuing acting ended before it even began. She came to the US with her husband and settled down in New Jersey. Meher was always restless and waited for an opportunity to break free. Then she became pregnant and had to give up on her acting passion till Sonya was born. Raghav was a doting father. He expected Meher to take care of the child. She had often expressed her desire to pursue her ambition, but Raghav put his foot down.

Meher had made a friend in Jenny, who was their neighbour. She was as old as Meher and was doing some stints in Broadway musicals. It so happened that Raghav had to travel to India for work. Meher was left alone to tend to their daughter who was then five-year-old. Being a mom and a housewife was frustrating. She knew she was not cut for the part.

One afternoon, Meher fed Sonya and put the cartoons for her. She then stepped out for smoke when she noticed Jenny with a cast on her leg, resting on the patio.

Jenny was on the way to rehearsals when she slipped and broke her ankle. She was sad that she won't be doing the musical. Then she asked Meher if she would like to take her place. The thought excited Meher. It was a once-in-a-lifetime opportunity, explained Jenny.

The next day, Meher dropped Sonya at the day-care and reached the rehearsal hall. David, who was directing the play, looked harried. His main lead had left the show for better opportunities on television. Just then, Meher walked in and stood nervously, taking in her surroundings.

David couldn't take his eyes off her. The woman was gorgeous and carried herself elegantly.

"Jenny sent me in her place. I suppose she spoke to you. I am Meher…"

David shook hands, taking in her beauty.

"I want you to read these lines for me. Can you do it?" David handed her a page off the script. Meher was shaking, not believing her luck.

In the next few moments, Meher had given an impressive performance. The team applauded, appreciating her acting skills. David offered her the lead. Things were happening in an unimaginable speed. It was as if the universe was waiting for Meher to make a move and finally her dream was turning into a reality.

Soon, Meher's face was on the poster of the musical. The shows ran house-full in New Jersey for a week. David decided to travel with the musical to other states in the US.

Suddenly, reality hit Meher. It was time for Raghav to return home. He would lose his cool if he knew that Meher had left Sonya in day-care to act in a musical. But the opportunity to pursue her dream was far more tempting than going back to an abusive husband and a child she had never wanted.

The day Raghav was supposed to return, Meher pinned a note with the number for day-care, wrote her goodbyes, packed her bags, and walked out with Sonya. She dropped Sonya at the day-care and joined David and his troupe. That was the last she had seen her daughter until…

Meher didn't get as much success as she had expected. She had an affair with David, and once it died down, he left her to fend for herself. Meher struggled to make ends meet. She did minuscule roles in television shows and lived off welfare. Many times, she thought of going home to Raghav and Sonya, but then changed her mind. She knew Raghav would never forgive her. Soon, age advanced, and work stopped coming. Giving up on her passion was the worst possible thing to happen to her. She took a job as a waitress at a restaurant. It was at the restaurant where she was serving some teenagers who were Indians that she heard about Sonya Rana, a famous Bollywood actress. Her pulse raced as she snatched the phone from one of the boys' hands. She was staring at a younger version of herself but more beautiful.

Since that day, Meher decided to get in touch with her estranged daughter. She read about Sonya who had gone on to become a star. The news about Raghav's death shocked her. She came across the news that Sonya Rana was in New Jersey. Meher went to see her. So, Raghav had not sold the house, she realised.

Meher caught a glimpse of Sonya and her breath nearly stopped. She was more stunning in person.. Meher wondered if Sonya would help her revive her acting career. She decided to confront Sonya, introduce herself as her mother, and beg for forgiveness. Meher kept a close watch on Sonya and followed her everywhere.

Then one day, she saw an opportunity when Sonya was visiting the local mall. Meher wondered if she should approach Sonya but then was sceptical of her reaction. Also, accompanying Sonya was a woman and a young girl. Meher thought they were part of her staff but when Sonya addressed the woman as 'mom', Meher felt a sting of disappointment. She had nearly abandoned her plan when she overheard the girls talking.

"Di…you don't have to worry about what mom would have to say about you going for a play. I will manage her. This is your chance. Go…"

The younger girl took the basket from her hands and made sure the coast was clear. Meher followed Sonya as she darted out through the main door and hopped into an SUV. Meher was happy to see that Sonya had inherited not only her looks but also her adventurous streak.

It was an opening night of the same Broadway musical in which Meher had starred decades ago and for which she had abandoned her daughter. It was not serendipity that her daughter had broken all the rules to come for the same musical. Meher took a ticket and entered the auditorium. To her surprise, it was empty. The show would start any moment, and before that, the audience needed to be in their seats thought Meher. Gingerly, Meher walked to her assigned row and was shocked to find Sonya occupying a seat.

"I knew you would follow me here. But what I had not expected was for the same musical to play at the same theatre after decades. This was the same musical for which you abandoned me at the daycare," Sonya said viciously.

Meher kept staring at her daughter. She had surrendered to her fate.

"It was not for the musical. I walked away from home to chase my dreams. But see where it brought me today." There was remorse in Meher's voice.

"Do you even know what the hell you put me through as a child? You went chasing your dreams, and here I was, left alone to fight for the people I loved. Fight for a home which you failed to give me. Fight for emotional security. During my entire growing up years, I have been fighting my fears."

Sonya struggled not to cry. She didn't want Meher to see how vulnerable she was. Meher wanted to take her in her arms hoping it would wipe away the years they had spent apart. But Sonya kept distance between them.

"I had noticed you the moment I saw you working at the gas station last year. Since then, I kept tabs on you. I had you followed. You chased one job after another. All these years, you didn't even bother to look for me or come get me."

Sonya seethed with anger. "Look where it has brought you today. The amount of destruction you let loose by walking away from me and dad is unimaginable."

Sonya thwarted any attempts by Meher to try to touch her.

"Please, let me take you in my arms…once. I beg you. I wanted to come back. I had decided to beg for forgiveness and accept whatever punishment or hell Raghav would put me through. Unfortunately, I realised it was too late. Raghav had already remarried."

"You are a liar. You wanted to come back because you failed. You didn't care about your daughter,"

Sonya's words stung Meher. She couldn't deny the fact that it was true.

Sonya walked past her. "Don't ever try to contact me. You were dead to me twenty years ago. And you will remain dead."

Sonya walked out as Meher crumpled the ticket in her palm and fell on the floor, sobbing.

Meher sat down to write a fresh letter to Sonya, begging for forgiveness, begging for one more chance to be her mom, begging to make everything right. But Sonya never replied.

Nineteen

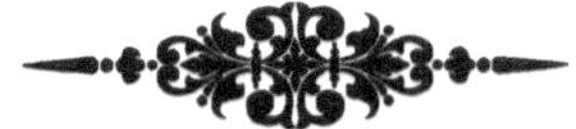

A look of nervousness flitted across Ramola's face as she sat across Dr. Kulkarni.

After the last session with Sonya, doctor had insisted to meet Ramola. Grudgingly, Ramola had accepted and here she was at his clinic.

Sonya had agreed to shoot with the chief assistant director for the last leg of the schedule. It was decided to take legal action against Mohan when they returned to India. That was comforting enough for Sonya.

"Tell me, Mrs. Rana, did Sonya ever tell you about the sexual abuse she was enduring in her own house as a child?" Dr. Kulkarni had decided he would get to the bottom of this. His line of treatment depended on what Ramola had to say.

Ramola looked a bit perturbed now. She had deliberated on the question for a long time. Her fears had come true.

Ramola cleared her throat, and after what seemed like ages, she finally spoke.

"Did she tell you this is what happened with her?" Ramola scoffed. "Sonya had always been highly imaginative as a child. I wouldn't believe a word she says." Ramola appeared flustered.

"Mrs. Rana, it is pertinent to know what steps you and your husband took to protect your daughter," Dr. Kulkarni was getting impatient with the web of lies the woman was weaving.

Ramola's gaze was fixated upon something on the wall. The nerve on her forehead twitched as it often did when faced with a difficult situation.

"Mrs. Rana… did you take the child in confidence and assure her of your support?" the doctor persisted.

"We waved it off as her fantasy. There was a baby in the house, and of course she was doing this to draw attention," Ramola wiped the sweat beads off her forehead and swatted away the doctor's query with a wave of her hand.

Dr. Kulkarni noticed she was nervous. The parents had messed up big time with their daughter. Ramola was protecting her brother while Raghav, as a father, had shown indifference towards Sonya, to a certain extent. Raghav was not here to give his version. Did he at least try to protect his daughter and failed in doing so? The birth mother had simply walked out. What an illustrious set of parents!

"After a certain time, you were aware of the abuse, weren't you?" Dr. Kulkarni took off his glasses and gave a grim look. "It makes you a party to the crime, Mrs. Rana."

Ramola closed her eyes, thinking about all the wrongs that happened in the past and how it had caught up with her. Ramola's face hardened as she opened her eyes and leaned forward.

We need to be on the same page here. Digging up the past will torment her more. Mistakes were made doctor. Not only by me but also her father and Meher. But now, there must be something we can do for her!" Ramola was pleading.

Dr. Kulkarni drew a deep breath, his gaze fixated on the sketch Sonya had handed him. It revealed a window, with a palm of a little girl pressed against the glass. It was a silent plea for help.

"After what she went through in Singapore - the hallucinations, alcohol, overdose and rape attempt, I think admitting her to psychiatric care will do good for her."

Ramola jerked up her head in shock.

"What are you saying? I can't just admit her to an asylum! Sonya is not some lay person. She is a star. People revere her. I hope you understand the ramifications of it all," Ramola angrily retorted.

"Mrs. Rana, Sonya needs psychiatric care. I am her therapist and I know what I am saying. You have to trust me. It is only for the good of your daughter," he said, exasperated at Ramola's outrage.

"Sonya's mental condition is deteriorating, and she is not getting any better, believe me," Dr. Kulkarni got up from his chair and started pacing the room.

Why was Ramola suddenly acting indifferent towards Sonya? Didn't she want her daughter to get a chance at leading a normal life. After what the girl had been through! Was she afraid that Sonya would lose out on being the number one star? It all boiled down to just one thing: money and fame!

"Try putting your daughter's life and her well-being first, Mrs. Rana, and then what I am saying will make sense," Dr. Kulkarni was now starting to lose patience. His heart went out to the distraught girl.

Ramola was silent for a long time.

"It will have to be in the US. I can't risk her career."

Ramola had leaned in Sonya's favour, and Dr. Kulkarni was more than happy to provide references.

Ramola left the clinic, thinking how she was going to convince Sonya and eventually Tania.

Twenty

The swing moved in a rhythm of its own. Sonya's head rested on Jay's shoulder.

"Sonya… Sonya…" Jay would often lose sense of time when he was with Sonya.

"Jay… what happened in Singapore… I so much wanted to speak to you then but what Kashyap did to me… I am so scared!" The thought awakened unpleasant memories in Sonya, as she rubbed her arms, irritated.

"Babe, there is nothing to fear. You are safe. Ask me why?" Sonya looked at him questioningly. "I am with you. I will not leave you alone hereafter." Jay kissed her forehead.

Jay picked up Sonya from the airport and drove her home. She appeared exhausted. Jay too believed Sonya should register a case of sexual harassment against Mohan Kashyap.

"Mom said registering a case against Kashyap will malign my reputation. Also, this incident is working in my favour. My movie is garnering a lot of attention before its release." Sonya sighed, going into Jay's arms.

Jay was shocked at Ramola's stand. This way, Sonya would never get the justice she deserved. Ramola normalised abuse in Sonya's life. Jay was aware he didn't have a say in this matter.

"I am tired. I don't want to go anywhere," Sonya said with a listless look in her eyes.

Jay placed his hand in hers, comforting Sonya. Was this Ramola's way of protecting her daughter? He frowned as he failed to understand Ramola. She was ready to send Sonya to a psychiatric facility. Maybe, at this moment, Sonya needed to get mentally strong.

"Sonya, your mom was talking about going to the States…for a while."

Sonya looked at him surprised. "Of course, it would be just for a while. Dr. Kulkarni has suggested treatment for you and…"

Sonya let go of Jay's hand, frowning. A feeling of abandonment wrapped its claws around her.

"You are jumping the ship, just like the others." Sonya's look hardened.

Jay thought he had lost her. Was this Ramola's evil machination to keep him out of Sonya's life? Did she seriously consider sending Sonya into a rehab? Jay was taken aback by his wayward thoughts. What was happening to him? Jay shook his head as if doing so would rid him of the negative thoughts.

It was his responsibility, as a 'friend', that's how Ramola put it, to gently break the news to Sonya and convince her. Jay understood Ramola was using him to get to Sonya. She was self-centred and selfish when it came to Sonya.

"I am not going anywhere, Jay," Sonya had moved away from him, arms crossed. She had a look of defiance.

"Why should I be the one to stuff myself with pills and take therapy? What about men like Kashyap and Vikram? Shouldn't they be going into a mental hospital or for that matter locked away forever?"

Jay considered his options. He didn't want to lose Sonya. It was a tricky situation that Ramola had put him in. He decided to take the risk and silence his inner voice. Jay walked over and gently turned Sonya towards him. He was gazing deep into Sonya's eyes. Today they were as cold as ice.

"Sonya, I have been wanting to tell you this for quite some time now." She listened, anxious and a little tense.

"We are best friends. We have known each other for a long time now and understand each other so well. I can read you like an open book, know what you want, feel your pain, and want to make you happy, see you smile."

Sonya looked at him, wondering where this was leading. Jay held her hand, placed it on his heart, and still looking at her, he went down on one knee.

"Sonya, I love you. I want to marry you," Jay's words held lots of promises.

Sonya knew he loved her, and she too loved him, but there was an emptiness in her. It was a vortex of unending misery and despair.

Sonya could feel the darkness enveloping her, destroying that tiny ray of hope. The darkness was cold and brutal. She could feel its grip on her heart; dark and hard. The monsters were closing in for the kill. She let go of Jay's hand.

"Have you ever gazed deep into your eyes... in the mirror?" Sonya had a vacant look in her eyes.

Jay's face clouded in confusion, reflecting the shadows of the night.

Sonya leaned in closer.

"I have and you know what I see?" Jay's heart skipped a beat.

"I see darkness in my eyes, Jay… darkness. It scares the hell out of me," Sonya whispered, glancing up at the clouds, pointing towards them. "This darkness is inside me; I can feel it. I don't want you to be a part of it."

"I love you, Jay… Go away, please… just go…" Sonya pushed him away and stepped back, away from Jay's outstretched hand, feeling something snap inside her.

"Sonya… babes, let me help you, please," Jay pleaded, but Sonya was in no mood to listen. Jay found himself standing outside her door. Sonya had locked herself in.

"Sonya… Sonya, open the door. Listen to me," Sonya switched on the music system in her room, turned up the volume, and lay on the bed, unmindful of the shouting and knocking.

Sonya wanted to drown the commotion; the ones inside her head and outside too. The noises within her were the real tormentors, murderers. The loud music blanketed them. She let the music wash over her. The voices in her head slowly dimmed.

Jay turned to find Ramola standing in the corridor. She shook her head, helplessness, and disappointment evident on her face.

"Aunty … she is not in a condition to listen," Jay looked away, trying hard to control his emotions.

"Aunty… I am sorry. I've got to go," Jay went away before he could break down.

Ramola sighed, despair taking over. He had been her only hope.

She wondered where all this was leading. Who could help her with this? As she mulled over this problem, a name crossed her mind. Of course, why had she not thought of it before!

Twenty One

The swing creaked as it swung up and then down. In her mind, it seemed to touch the sky as it swung up, carrying Sonya sprawled on it. Her robe trailed below, swelling with the wind. The dark skies closed in, hovered around her and hissed. She had stayed closeted in her room for the past couple of days. The phone had rung many times. She had ignored them. There were calls from Tania, Jay, and Ramola who was at the door too, knocking persistently. Sonya had let the battery drain out completely. Her phone was dead, and she wished she were dead too.

Sonya pushed the swing a little harder; her legs almost touching the balcony railing. If she let go of the swing and pushed hard, she would fall to her death. A figure splattered on the asphalt below, blood everywhere, a gory sight. Death will mark the end of her suffering, misery, the darkness, the voices, and the turmoil within.

Sonya sighed, stopped pushing the swing, and just lay there for a while, in oneness with the tranquility within. It was not to last long.

Suddenly, Sonya sat up, eyes wide with terror, body stiffened, wary of a presence. She could see shadows closing in on her. She stepped back, but they were quick, the vile creatures. They had pushed her to the railing. She looked down and saw dark shadows lining the pavement. They were slowly creeping up towards her. As she leaned forward, the shadows assumed forms of men and women, clenching and unclenching their fists, grinding their teeth. The eyes were empty sockets with blood oozing out, making them more hideous. These monsters tried to grab Sonya and pull her into their world; a deep, dark void. She screamed.

"Leave me alone... leave me alone... I am not coming with you," she screamed, helpless and scared. The monsters were stubborn. They did not heed to her pleas.

"Tania... Tania... help me... Jay... please... I need you. Where are you? I can't take it anymore." Sonya cried out, closing the balcony door.

The monsters had put on a nocturnal dance. She knew they would not leave without her. Sonya staggered to her bedside drawer and rummaged through its contents.

A few seconds later, she came up with a bottle. Unscrewing the cap, Sonya drank neat. The amber liquid burned her throat, causing tears to fill her eyes. It hit her empty stomach, erupting in a ball of fire, the pain shooting to her head. Sonya had stopped feeling anything… hunger, love, loneliness except fear. The pain felt good.

The monsters had gone for the time being, replaced by the voices in her head which attacked her with vengeance, breaking her mind, tormenting her soul. Sonya strayed into insanity and back, eyes listless, lost, but not dead.

The images came vividly, in flashes, then blurred into a ball of colours. She was hallucinating.

Sonya rang Jay's doorbell; once, twice, thrice, and frantically banged the door. She could hear footsteps getting closer, murmurs; angry and anxious.

The door opened, and Sonya wheezed past Sandhya, who was surprised. Soon it was replaced with kindness and worry. Why wasn't she born to Sandhya? Her life would have had some meaning, little semblance of peace.

"Sonya… what happened? Is everything all right?" Sandhya could see that Sonya was distraught.

Sonya wanted to collapse in Sandhya's arms, give into the voice which oozed kindness and warmth. Instead, she went numb. Past few days Sonya had been in and out of darkness. Her thoughts had warped the concept of time. When she came to her senses, for that miniscule moment, she heard Sandhya urging her to speak, shaking her awake.

"Aunty, I need to speak with Jay," The words tumbled out faster as if it was in race with the time her thoughts had construed.

Sandhya patted her arm gently. "Sonya… why don't you sit for a second. I will get you something to drink…"

Sonya brushed her hand away, weary of a comforting touch. "Aunty, I don't have time. I really need to speak with Jay… now," Sonya's voice had urgency. She looked in the direction of Jay's room.

"Sonya, Jay is at work. Talk to me, sweetheart," Sonya looked at Sandhya and for a moment, gave into the temptation. Good things had the habit of drifting away from her. Sonya choked down a sob.

"I wanted to talk to him. I so much wanted to…" Sonya was exhausted with the games her mind was playing with her.

"Jay did call you. He even came by your house, but he said you refused to meet him." Sandhya was patting her hand.

Sonya appeared confused. She tried hard to recollect but her mind drew blank. Then a thought struck her. Was she here or was this a trick conjured by her mind? Sonya staggered back, no longer able to fathom reality. It terrified her.

Suddenly Sonya walked to the door, hesitated. When she turned, Sandhya gasped.

When Sonya turned, Sandhya gasped, a chill creeping up her spine. There was something haunting in her gaze. They say that the eyes are the windows to the soul, eternal and unchanging, yet Sonya's eyes bore the weight of a thousand unspoken horrors. It was as if they had witnessed the darkest corners of existence, reflecting a lifetime steeped in torment and despair. Each glance was a silent scream, a reminder that some souls are forged in suffering, their depths fathomless and chilling.

"Aunty, could you please not tell Jay that I had come over to meet him? I don't want to mess up his life."

Saying this, Sonya hurried out, not waiting for Sandhya's answer who seemed to be in a shock.. Sonya did not wait for the elevator; instead, she took the long flight of steps.

✳ ✳ ✳

Sonya sat down, her back to the bed. She toyed with the knife in her hands, dazed.

It all came back to her. It had been a month since she had met Jay. Her thoughts went back to the evening on the terrace when Jay had told her he loved her, and then she had pushed him away… out of her life. She looked at her reflection in the mirror, cursing her fate.

"It was not me who pushed the love of my life away," Sonya sobbed, screaming in pain. "It is the evil in me. I hate you… I hate you." Sonya picked up the remote next to her and flung it at the mirror. There were glass shards everywhere in the room.

Somewhere in the depth of her mind where light shone, Sonya was aware, she was closing all doors. There was no one to go to now. The knife glinted as it caught the first rays of sun. Sonya held the knife in her hands. Its blade now resting on her wrist. Sonya closed her eyes, took a deep breath, and felt its touch; cold and sharp.

"I must get rid of this evil in me. You've got to go…"

"Di… Sonya Di… it's me, Tania," followed by loud banging and pleas.

Sonya's eyes flew open. Was Tania here or was her mind playing games with her? No…no, it can't be.

Then she heard Tania once again calling, pleading with her to open the door. Sonya hid the knife under the pillow and walked towards the door.

Sonya opened the door and peeked out. Tania nearly broke into tears on seeing the frail figure, sunken eyes, hollow cheeks, and a vacant look.

Sonya ran into her arms, sobbing, her body trembling with spasms. Tania, hugged her, patting her comfortingly.

"I drove Jay away… from my life. He will never come back now. Oh! Tania, what have I done?" Sonya cried.

Tania consoled her, murmuring reassuring words in her ears.

Later, as Sonya soaked in a warm bubble bath, Tania handed her a glass of cold water.

"Di, you are coming with me to the States," Sonya gave her a befuddled look. She opened her mouth to protest.

"I am not asking here. As we speak, your bags are being packed. Your tickets are already booked. Mom is coming with us too," Tania sounded like an elder sister, all grown up and matured. Sonya looked at her admiringly.

"I trust you, little one. I trust you with my life," Sonya mumbled as Tania looked on, worried.

Sonya looked haggard. She had lost her charm. Ramola had called Tania two days ago, saying that Sonya had locked herself in her room since last week.

"And you are calling me now? What's wrong with you? I did try to call Di, but she did not answer. I assumed she was busy with her work." Tania's pulse was racing. She had gotten home from her part-time job in the college library and had settled in bed for the night.

"I didn't know what to do. Have you girls ever given a thought to my mental well-being?" Ramola asked flustered.

Tania gasped. "Why do you make everything about yourself? It is Sonya who needs our help."

Ramola grunted her disappointment. "I spoke to you about admitting Sonya to a psychiatric care in the States. Well, arrangements are done, but Sonya refuses to listen. She did not even listen to Jay. I am truly worried," Ramola was frustrated.

By the time she finished speaking to Ramola, Tania was dressed and packed to leave for the airport.

A day later, Tania arrived, severely jet-lagged and exhausted but concerned for her elder sister.

"What did you survive on for the last eight days?" Tania asked as she shampooed Sonya's hair.

"I lost track of time. I don't feel hungry at all." Sonya made more bubbles.

Tania rolled her eyes at the bottles lying around the room.

"Oh! Yeah, while we were worried sick outside, you were having a party in your room!" Tania glared at her. She was angry at Sonya for causing tensions and worries. She was angry because Sonya was hurting within and she, Tania, could not help.

Sonya murmured her apologies and looked away.

"Di ... I care for you. I love you and I can't see you wasting away like this! You know it, don't you?" Sonya did not look at her but nodded her head.

"Promise you won't give up? We will get through this together." Tania took her hand and gave it a gentle squeeze.

Sonya tried hard to fight off tears. She nodded her head as Tania hugged her.

"Tania…It hurts…" Sonya cried like a child. Tania got into the tub and cradled Sonya in her arms, soothing her fears with kind and assuring words.

"I promise I will behave. I will do exactly what you want me to," Sonya sobbed.

Tania wanted to trust her sister. A feeling of dread seeped into her heart. Was she losing Sonya?

PART II

Six Months Later

Sujoy Sarkar's production house resembled a frenzy of activity. With the announcement of a new film going on floors in six months, pre-production work was in full swing. There were auditions being held, meetings with the casting director, dates of stars to be managed, dress rehearsals, and finalising locations underway.

Sonya sat in the conference room, checking her nails, tucking her ginger hair behind her ears, nervous. Five years ago, she had come to this very office; auditioned for a role and had bagged the film. In the first week of its release, the film became a super hit at the box office and Sonya became a star overnight. She was only 19 then.

Three months later, Sonya had another hit. The gorgeous, vivacious Sonya was the cynosure of Sujoy Sarkar. Today, oddly, she had to wait in the conference room for a full one hour before Sujoy made an appearance.

Things were different back then. Sujoy would wait for Sonya to come to his office, request her for public appearances, and show her off to the world on his arm. "Maybe he is busy or maybe he is avoiding her." The last thought made her restless. Suddenly, she felt short of breath. Sonya gasped for air. She was experiencing one of those panic attacks which doctors at the psychiatric care in New Jersey had warned her about.

Sonya dipped into her handbag and removed Zapiz 25, and placed it beneath her tongue, letting it work its magic. It will eventually send a calming message to the brain. The doctors had prescribed it for her in case she needed it. Ten minutes passed and Sonya sensed the flutter in her heart had slowed down, her breathing normalised. She once again glanced at the closed door, expecting Sujoy to walk in. She gave him two more minutes and then picked up her handbag and got up to leave when the door was thrown open and in walked Sujoy.

"Hey Sonya… how have you been?" Sujoy had a big grin on his face.

No apologies for making her wait, no remorse, Sonya noted with sadness creeping up inside her. He hugged Sonya, held her at arm's length, and looked at her.

"You're looking great, girl! This break has done you good," Sujoy nodded at her, locking his arm in hers and walked her to his cabin.

Sujoy noted she had lost a considerable amount of weight. She looked pretty but frail. The glamour had waned, Sujoy sighed.

As she walked through the office corridors, Sonya could see her pictures were replaced by some newcomer, whom Sujoy was launching in his next film. Sonya felt her heart take a wee tumble there, but she composed her thoughts and even managed to smile at Sujoy's secretary who waved at her in the lobby. Was that an awkward wave? Did this walk mean Sujoy's goodbye? Was he trying to convey some kind of message by making sure she saw the pictures of the new girl he was introducing to Bollywood?

Sonya had spent two months at the New Jersey Psychiatric Care as per Dr. Kulkarni's directive. When she came back to India, she was in better control of her emotions, was off alcohol, and off drugs. The doctors had advised her to take baby steps to recovery.

Sonya nervously looked around and found distraction in the young girls assembled in the office lobby as they redid their makeup and smoothed their revealing outfits. The boys smoked and talked, their eyebrows raised and hands moving in the air, nodding their heads in nervous apprehension. Some girls joined them, bumming cigarettes, each gathering courage from one another, trying to calm their nerves. Sonya frowned, remembering how she had taken the stage as if she belonged. No one could replace her fierceness. Life had taken a wrong turn for her and she remained stuck on the turnstile.

Some of them had noticed Sonya, and they whispered to each other, casting curious in her direction.

Welcome to the world of fucked-up stars! Sonya thought, rolling her eyes and smirking.

Later, Sonya set down her coffee and looked questioningly at Sujoy. Desperation was evident in her eyes and she felt a wave of shame grip her. Sujoy was busy checking schedules on his laptop.

"Sujoy... I am back after a short hiatus. I am feeling much better now, in control," Sujoy looked up, nodded his head, smiled, and went back to his laptop.

Sonya clenched and unclenched her fingers, pursed her lips, and looked around at the trophies lining the mantel behind him. There were a couple of them from the films she had worked on with him.

"Together we have created magic, and I think it's time we give it a shot," Sonya said, suddenly feeling euphoric. But Sujoy's lack of interest was dampening her spirit.

Sujoy nodded his head, still engrossed with his laptop, distracted. She knew Sujoy very well. He was transparent when it came to emotions. He could never lie.

Sujoy took a break from his work and turned to Sonya. "Sonya, I trust your capabilities or else I would never have given you your first break." He reached out for her hand and looked forlornly at her. Sonya nodded her head in agreement.

"I want you to take it slow. There is no reason for you to become insecure. Just because I am not signing you for a film, it doesn't mean you are no longer a star, or you do not mean anything to me." Sujoy's words were soothing and gentle.

Instead of finding comfort in his words, Sonya felt unease creep inside her. A shadow began clouding her heart and her mind.

Sonya suddenly got up, forcing Sujoy to let go of her hand. She smoothed her dress, wove a hand through her tresses and tried to put on a brave smile.

"That's alright, I got my answer. I am neither insecure nor desperate as you might put it or the press who has written me off. I am not. I am still a star. You tasted success because of me." Sonya burst out angry, pacing the room. "Don't forget," she waved a finger at him.

"Sonya ... listen to me. It is not what you think..." Sujoy tried to reach out to her but she flinched.

Sujoy was not confident whether Sonya would carry an entire film on her shoulders. Her long absence from the limelight and admission in psychiatric care had created a buzz in the film world. The press had written her off. They now referred to her as a 'fallen star'. Signing her for a movie now meant a risk that he was unwilling to take at this stage. He was now an established producer. It was the truth. Sonya had made him a star producer and now he didn't want to risk all of it.

Sonya turned, her eyes as cold as ice, freezing Sujoy. "You abandoned me when I needed you the most. You will not hear from me now. Goodbye, Sujoy. Wish you luck."

Sonya put on her aviators, took a deep breath, and walked out, head held high as people stared at her, whispered and nudged each other.

"Jay, it's the end of the road for me," Sonya said dejectedly, looking at the young girl walking the tightrope. The girl was emancipated. Sonya wondered if she had proper meals. If she was fat, would she be able to walk the rope? Her hands outstretched on either side, gaze straight ahead, carefully clenching the rope between toes as she took a step ahead. A scene out of one of the road shows put up by the gypsies. This girl had struck a perfect balance in life which was terribly lacking in hers, Sonya thought.

Jay offered Sonya coffee as they sat in the car, watching the girl jump down from the rope with a triumphant smile. Her younger brother went about collecting money from the people gathered there while her mother played a tiny drum.

"Life is not a cakewalk but a rope walk, one misstep and you come crashing down, " Sonya was now looking at the girl sitting on the pavement, looking up at the rope which she had just walked on.

"You know what, babes? I am not very fond of this philosophical side of yours," Jay scrunched his nose in disapproval.

"Come here," he pulled her into his arms.

Sonya did not resist, tucking away her wayward tresses, his thumb grazing her cheek as he stared deep into her eyes.

"I have been wanting to take you dancing, show you how much I love you," Jay gently kissed her. Sonya kissed back.

"I love you, babes, and I want us to be together forever," Jay entwined his fingers in hers, one hand going around her waist, not taking his gaze away from her face.

"Marry me, Sonya. I am saying this once again and will keep saying it again and again," Jay said. For a moment, Jay thought he had lost her as Sonya just stared at him, the blue in her eyes getting intense.

"Look at me, Jay. What do you see?" Jay was taken aback.

"This is not the real me. This is not the Sonya you love. The Sonya you love was beautiful, happy, not broken."

"Are you willing to walk with a broken person by your side?"

Jay was about to say something, but she silenced him by placing her finger on his lips.

"Jay, listen to me. You have had an awesome start. Don't give up everything for me," Sonya said as she got out of the car and stood leaning on the door, her arms crossed over her chest.

"Don't push me away Sonya. Give us one chance." Jay pleaded, coming to stand next to her, holding her hand.

Slowly, Sonya withdrew her hand from his and stepped back.

"Believe me, you don't want to be with me in my darker times."

Why was Jay not able to comprehend her feelings?

"Life is beautiful, Sonya. Give it a chance," Jay said, noting a faraway look in Sonya's eyes.

"Sadly, life never gave me that chance, Jay. It screwed up big time," Sonya bit her lip, sadness bordering her tone.

"Don't talk nonsense. Trust me, Sonya, we will make it work. There are a hundred Sujoys in this world who are willing to work with you. You are still a star, babes," Jay said with conviction that Sonya was tempted to believe him for a moment. Jay saw a ray of hope flash on her face, but it faded as fast as it had come.

Sonya looked at her watch. "I should be going, Jay. It's late. Time has never been in my favour and trusting someone has not been my strongest fortitude."

"Hey babes, we can still make things work, put everything behind us... just this once!" Jay held on, not wanting to let go of Sonya. There was still hope that Sonya would come around.

"I think I will go back to New Jersey. I need a break. I am tired," Jay reluctantly let go of Sonya.

"Let me at least drop you home." Jay implored to which Sonya smiled.

"I need to find my way home...alone." She turned and then to herself, she said in a heart wrenching tone, "If there really is a home waiting for me."

Sonya had not sounded that happy this morning when he had called. Jay thought he would make her understand, get her around to understand his perspective and make her believe in his promise.

Jay knew very well how stubborn Sonya could be! Once her mind was made up, she would see it through to the end. At times, her words made no sense to Jay, but deep down, he knew she was hurting, and he felt helpless. He could do nothing to alleviate her pain.

✴ ✴ ✴

My Beloved Jay,

It's 2:00 am and I lie awake, staring at the ceiling. Everything appears calm outside, but my mind is full of turmoil. There are noises in my head, thoughts coming and going at their own will. My heart wells up with anguish and fear. I try to calm down, take stock of things but the world is whirling madly around me.

Are these voices in my head just my imagination or a product of a meandering mind? Why can't I block them, fight them, but instead, I let them take over me, surrendering myself to their dark side.

Why am I telling all this to you? It's nearly been a month since we last met. Many a time I thought of calling you, speaking with you, meeting you for old times' sake! What good will that do? Inside, I am hurting a lot, and I don't want you to suffer with me. I don't deserve you, Jay, but you will always remain special to me.

Jay, besides Tania, you were the only one who understood me, cared about my needs. I don't want to mess with your life anymore. My mind is in turmoil. I very well know I am heading towards disaster, so it's better if you stay away.

The world might think you deserted Sonya when she needed you the most. I care what the world thinks or does! I can take care of myself., I am not crying ... These tears make me seem so helpless and have weakened me from within. I hate myself; I hate everyone around me, and I hate my guts. This darkness will kill me one day. Then I won't have any more strength left in me. That day will be the last day of my life.

Jay, I wish you a good life and pray you are always surrounded by good people who love you and have the best for you in their thoughts. I am coming to the end of my journey, and I find myself standing alone at the crossroads. The path ahead is a treacherous one. I know that is not the path marked for me by my destiny. I just need to turn my back and take the path that will lead me to oblivion.

Goodbye my beloved. If God permits, we will meet in the next life.

Love you always.

Yours forever

Sonya

The diary slipped from her hands as Sonya drifted off into a medicated sleep. A few minutes later, as she fell asleep, she was awakened by loud knocks. It was her mom.

"Sonya… Sonya… open the door. Sonya… Sonya… dear…" Ramola continued to knock.

Sonya knew her mother would never back off, and if the need arises, she will break down the door. Sonya sat on the bed, her hands covering her ears, trying to block her mom's sound.

Everyone in the house was wary about her locking herself in. Finally, Sonya opened the door. Her mom entered, looking all flustered.

"Don't ever do this again, Sonya…" Ramola stopped mid-sentence, covered her face with the palm of her hand, scrunching her nose. Her eyes searching for something, a look of indignation flashed across her face.

"Sonya … you have been drinking … again?" Ramola asked, her voice bordering on anger. Sonya stared at her listlessly. Sighing, Ramola started picking up the things strewn on Sonya's bed.

"Sonya … what's happening? Why are you behaving like this?" Before she could see the diary, Sonya hurriedly stashed it in the closet, in its hiding place.

"Mom… I am fine…" Sonya replied through clenched teeth. Nowadays, it was becoming difficult for Sonya to hide her temper.

As Ramola folded the bed sheets, Sonya lunged for the knife, hiding it swiftly. Ramola threw her a surprised look.

"I am really worried about you, Sonya."

What I need is for you to love me with an open heart, Sonya's eyes pleaded, following Ramola's every movement.

"Let's go see Dr. Kulkarni. Last time we went, you walked out half-way through the sessions. Why are you doing this to yourself? Did you take those pills he prescribed?" Ramola searched her face for an answer.

Why did my mother abandon me? Am I so bad? Am I a burden to you too? Can't you love me the way a mother loves her daughter.

"Are you taking drugs? I hope not…" Ramola's eyes wandered around the room for any tell-tale signs that could suggest so.

"Mom… I don't want to talk about this. Can we do this some other time?" Sonya stood before the mirror, combing her hair as if it were a task to fill up her time.

"Sonya … I hope you remember we are meeting Mr. Patel today."

Noticing the blank look on her daughter's face, Ramola said, "Patel, that movie producer we met at the party last week. He called yesterday. He and the scriptwriter will be coming over for narration in a couple of hours. You get ready."

Ramola did not bother to wait for Sonya's answer and left the room.

Later

Sonya was furious, and her anger was directed at Patel, who cowered in a corner, mumbling something inaudible and wiping sweat off his brow. The writer just sat there, horrified, not knowing how to react. It was probably his first stint at story narration.

"Who do you think you are? I will tell you… you are a piece of stinking shit.. You have the audacity to offer me a B-grade film! Me? Sonya Rana…? I am a star… I am still a star." Sonya picked up the vase and waved it over their heads. Her eyes appeared bloodshot, and her body shook with rage. Her confidence wavered for a bit as she spoke but soon regained composure. She flung the vase on the wall behind them, sending the men scurrying for their life.

Sonya was trembling with anger as Ramola implored her to calm down.

Sonya turned to Ramola, who for a second thought that Sonya was going to attack her, but instead, Sonya threw a hurt look at her and went to her room.

She heard her mother apologising to Patel and the main door shut, then footsteps in her direction. She knew what would follow later. This was not the first time her mother had fixed a meeting with a producer offering her B-grade films. It was happening repeatedly.

When Sonya saw her mom standing at the door, she simply turned away to stare at the walls who had been her constant companions. At least they didn't hurt her or cause any pain.

Ramola was not about to give up.

"Sonya, your behaviour is not at all civil. It's pathetic! You think throwing tantrums will get you good banners? You need to be visible to people out there. If you want to confine yourself to these four walls, fine, but public memory is short. In a matter of time, you will be forgotten and replaced by a new girl. This happened with you at Sujoy Sarkar's office and will happen again. You need to convince people that you are back on your feet," Sonya's behaviour had undergone a drastic change as she was convinced of her fading stardom.

"Why don't you give up? I am tired of pleasing these B-grade directors and producers you line up every day. Get out of here." Sonya banged the door shut in Ramola's face.

Ramola shook her head in shock, nodding in frustration and anger. "Fine... do whatever you want. I am not staying here with you now. Don't speak to me unless you are willing to apologise. You stay away from my daughter, you crazy girl." Ramola said a bit harshly. But there was no response from Sonya.

Sonya only hugged herself tighter and sobbed. Her body curled into a tight ball. She had mentally shut herself off from the outside world.

A few minutes later, Sonya heard the main door closing. She shuddered. A feeling of loneliness enveloped her as she sat on the bed, rocking her body, staring into a vacant space ahead. She hummed the lullaby Tania sang to her.

The shadows shifted at the windows as Sonya's worst fears came true. Sonya heard voices, people talking about her, criticising her, laughing at her. Sonya tried to block them by covering her ears, but they became stronger. She rushed to the balcony and flung it open, hoping in vain they would go away but the sight that met her eyes terrified her further. Below, she could see people with microphones and cameras in their hands. Slowly, to Sonya's horror, they morphed into multi-headed monsters trying to make a grab at her. Sonya screamed, wildly flailing her arms, trying to free herself from the monster's grip that had by now merged into one big-headed monster who opened his mouth to swallow her. Sonya stepped back in horror and shut the door.

Terrified, she sat in a corner waiting for the horrible voices to subside. She could still see the monster's shadow dancing outside in the balcony. Sonya shut her eyes and covered her ears, wishing for the monsters to go away. Sonya knew these monsters were here to haunt her for the rest of her life, and there was only one way that she could escape from them.

Sonya took a swig from the bottle and sat staring at the box where she had hidden the knife.

It was time to face the diabolical within!

Sonya stepped into the balcony through the French doors. A soft breeze caressed her face. It was late evening. The city had come to life, lights killing the darkness, houses filled with happy sounds, but Sonya had blocked the sound of happiness from her life.

The city had a blanket of stars pulled over it. Never had they shone so brightly! Sonya thought, gazing up, as she lay down on the swing, staring at the multitude of stars shining above her. She held the knife to the light, and the blade glistened in the dark. The monster waited and watched. It was time to end the evil in her, free her soul, and feel what happiness is! She was not going to let Vikram win this time. She was not going to let him have the pleasure of tormenting her, killing her bit by bit. The diabolical had to die tonight!

Sonya heard laughter from her neighbour's house. In some house below her, a comedy show played where the people erupted in laughter. These were the sinful temptations that bespoke life. She shut her eyes, trying to ignore the sounds and concentrate on her breathing, a technique she had perfected during her sessions with her therapist.

"What the mind perceives and believes, it achieves. Calm your nerves and focus on every breath you take."

Sonya knew it was now time to apply Dr. Kulkarni's teachings. Her mind had always rebelled, but now she had to rein it in.

In this relentless pursuit of survival, death emerges as a paradoxical saviour.

Sonya's hold tightened over the knife.

The monster stared at her, unsure. Sonya wanted it all to end soon. A few moments more in this world and then there won't be any monsters terrorising her. She could feel the adrenaline rushing through her body.

The throbbing pain in her heart and mind was like a hammer. How beautiful it would be to be pain free, thought Sonya, wryly.

It will be a matter of time before I bleed out, she thought, feeling a tightening in her chest.

Sonya gazed down at the people who appeared to be an earnest part of the living world.

It's time for me to go. The thoughts came and went rapidly through her fuzzy brain.

My dying is not going to make any difference to this world. Jay will surely grieve for me. But will move on in life.

I am sorry, Jay... I love you and will continue loving you.

Tania, the light of my life...I will carry you with me.

Sonya was mumbling. Every breath caused a spasm to erupt in her chest. Her dress stuck to her body, her hair damp with sweat, mixed with fear and anticipation of death. She had spent her life in loneliness and despair and now at the time of death, nothing had changed. She was alone. She took in a few more rapid breaths when the door to her room was thrown open.

✳ ✳ ✳

Arjun Deshmukh reached the supposed crime scene after receiving a call from the control room about a possible suicide. He was surprised to know the house belonged to Sonya Rana. He had been here before. He hoped she was alive. He had inspected many crime scenes and came across dead bodies, but nothing prepared him for this. Sonya lay on the swing, blood pooled around her hand, which swung like a pendulum, her fingertips grazing the floor, ever so lightly. Her long, luscious hair splayed across her face. He noticed the knife lying nearby. Ramola was screaming and crying, creating a ruckus. He had her moved to another room. Arjun didn't see Tania at first but then noticed her peeping from behind her bedroom door, terrified. Ramola came screaming towards him, yelling accusation at Jay Malhotra, as he was the last person to see Sonya alive.

***

Ten Days Later

Jay is escorted to the courtroom, flanked on both sides by the police. Sandhya and Rishabh follow him with their lawyer. It's a total media circus out there as mikes are being shoved in their faces and flashbulbs explode. Jay is tight-lipped, as instructed by his lawyer, Mr. Acharya.

Rishabh arranged for the best lawyer he knew and assured Jay he would get him out, no matter what.

As the trio walked to the courtroom, one of the journalists, a young girl from a news channel, managed to break through the barrier of close friends and family around Sandhya and pushed a piece of paper into her hands. Her movements were frantic, and there was a sense of discreetness in her behaviour. For a moment, their eyes met, anxiousness and urgency screaming through them, and the next moment, the girl disappeared into the sea of people. Sandhya, distracted, shoved the piece of paper into her handbag and walked to the courtroom tensed about the fate of her only son.

It pained Sandhya to see her son being treated like a criminal in court. She spotted Ramola on the left with Tania, deep in conversation with their lawyer. Sandhya tried to catch her attention and for a split second thought she had glanced in her direction.

Ramola had seen Sandhya and knew she wanted to talk, but this was not the time to talk or make amends. She had lost her daughter, and according to the letter found in Sonya's possession, Jay was to be blamed.

Sandhya was clueless as to what was going through Ramola's mind. Ramola had been so nice to Jay and trusting around Sonya. What had happened for the sudden change to come over her? Lots of thoughts were going through Sandhya's mind, and she found herself feeling helpless and alone.

The courtroom was damp and dingy. Rains continued to lash outside, but the media braved it all, waiting for the verdict on the Jay versus Sonya suicide case. Sandhya's mind trailed off to that fateful evening. Jay's best friend, Rohit, had stormed into the house ten days ago, with worry and fear etched on his face.

"Jay, Sandhya aunty…" Rohit was breathless by the time he walked in through the doors.

"*Hey… what happened? Look at you,*" *Jay said, taking in Rohit's drenched look. It was pouring outside, and from the looks of it, Rohit had left his home without an umbrella.*

"*There is bad news, Jay,*" *Rohit, tongue-tied, just stared at his friend, wondering the best possible way to break Sonya's news.*

"*What bad news?*" *Jay had just gotten home from a client meeting.. He had planned to head straight for the shower.*

"*Sonya is dead. They are saying she committed suicide,*" *Jay slumped on the couch, shocked.*

"*Rohit… what? How did this happen?*" *Sandhya's palms broke into sweat, and she started blabbering. "Are you sure? I mean…*"

"*She cut her wrist. Her mother found her lying in a pool of blood. It was too late to take her to the hospital.*"

"*Why did they leave her alone? Ramola knew her mental condition very well,*" *Sandhya said to herself, dabbing sweat from her forehead.*

Rohit's words seemed to be coming from miles away. Why had this young girl taken her life? Sandhya looked at Jay, who was devastated by the news. What more this child have to endure at such a young age, Sandhya thought.

Sandhya had no idea Jay's life was about to take a turn for the worse.

"All rise." Sandhya's train of thoughts was broken by the judge's arrival in court.

This was no courtroom like the one Sandhya had seen in movies. This was for real. It had a depressing feel to it. The wooden benches gave out a dank smell. Framed pictures of Indian freedom fighters hung on the walls, held together by nails that had rusted around their edges. Rainwater had seeped in through the corners, forming water bubbles on the ceiling, causing the paint to flake. Sandhya shuddered at the thought of waiting in this room for more than five minutes. Then she looked at Jay who stood with a vacant look in his eyes, awaiting the verdict for a crime he had not committed.

Sandhya had not in her wildest dreams thought that her son would have to witness the horrors of a police station and courts.

This morning, Sandhya was returning home from the temple. She sensed someone was watching her. She turned and checked twice but not a peep. That weird feeling remained with her until she came home. As soon as she entered, a couple of policemen followed her, asking for Jay.

"We are here for Jay Malhotra for abetting Sonya Rana's suicide We are taking him in for questioning."

Sandhya was too shocked to react. It was only when Jay protested that she came to her senses.

"Why are you taking my son? He has nothing to do with Sonya's death," Sandhya tugged at Jay's hand. "Let him go."

Jay seemed scared and confused at what was happening. One minute he was within the safe confines of his house, and the next minute he was in handcuffs. It was totally unbelievable, he thought to himself.

"Believe me, sir; I have nothing to do with Sonya's death," Jay pleaded.

Random thoughts crossed his mind: I had plans today. I was supposed to be at the gym now. My trainer, no doubt, would be mad at me for being late. I had asked mom to make my favourite dinner; roast chicken and veggies. What about my meeting with the new client tomorrow? Geez, what was happening? What have you done, Sonya? Why end it all so suddenly?

Jay dejectedly resigned himself to his fate, as he was loaded into the police van. Sandhya put in a call to Rishabh at the office, informing him about the arrest. Sandhya saw the police van drive away with Jay in tow. Sandhya was literally in tears and looked around helplessly.

"They took our Jay. They are holding him for Sonya's suicide," Sandhya broke down as soon as she saw Rishabh.

"There is very little time to be lost, Sandhya. I have called Mr. Acharya. He is the best defence lawyer in town," Rishabh murmured as they got in their car.

"This is happening for real. Only Sonya knows the truth. My son is innocent." A look of determination came across Sandhya's face as she dialled a number.

"Who are you calling, Sandhya?" Rishabh looked at her, confused.

"Pick up... please, for God's sake, Ramola, please pick up the phone," she kept dialling, but her call went unanswered.

"It is Ramola who has filed a case against Jay! Do you expect her to speak with you?" Rishabh nodded his head in disbelief as Sandhya looked away.

Sandhya leaned back, letting her tears flow freely. Rishabh reached out; gave her hand a reassuring pat. Ramola's deception was too painful for Sandhya.

The judge, Mr. Nabar, a middle-aged man, listened patiently to the case put forward by Suresh Saxena, representing Ramola Rana. Mr. Nabar, was in his early fifties, with salt-and-pepper hair defining his large forehead.

His brows creased at the mention of a young girl committing suicide after being spurned by her lover.

"Your honour, Jay Malhotra is responsible for the death of my client's daughter Sonya Rana, who was a reputed actress. She committed suicide on 27th June in her house by slashing her wrists and bled to death," Saxena said loudly enough for everyone in the courtroom, including the media. A murmur went up in the court like a wave riding on sea one stormy night.

Nabar shuffled in his seat, adjusting his robe and cleared his throat. He looked at the young lawyer in the eyes and asked, "I have read up on the case. Present the necessary evidence please." Nabar was restless and in a tearing hurry to get away.

Saxena, as if waiting for his cue, withdrew a letter from his file and handed it to the judge.

"Sir, this is the letter written by the deceased Sonya Rana, sometime before she committed suicide. Here, she clearly holds Jay Malhotra responsible for her death."

The judge adjusted his gold-rimmed glasses and started reading the contents of the letter. The media was eager to get their hands on the letter. Ramola had a smug look on her face. Jay waited nervously, shuffling his feet, shaking from the unexpected turn of events. He had spent a restless few days in lockup and dreaded going back.

Nabar having finished reading the letter, returned it to the lawyer.

"Order, order... I want you all to maintain silence in my court," Nabar banged the mallet thrice on the table, a little sternly. He knew most people present in the court felt indifferent to Sonya's dying. The media was hungry for news.

Then the judge turned to Mr. Acharya. "You may present your defence."

Acharya walked to the centre of the courtroom and rubbed his hands together. He looked at Ramola, who was staring straight ahead, and then at Jay. The judge shuffled once more in his seat at the endless gimmicks put up by the lawyers for media's sake.

"Why is he taking so much time? I have dozens of hearings lined up and then a relaxing weekend in Goa." Judge Nabar tried hard not to smile.

It was going to be a perfect getaway with his mistress. His wife had gone to the US for her nephew's wedding. Judge Nabar could not wait to get out of this dank smelling courtroom. He was planning for a good retirement... soon.

What seemed like an eternity, Acharya had finally begun his defence!

"Your honour, my client Jay Malhotra is wrongly accused of abetting Sonya Rana's suicide. He does not stand to benefit from her death. Jay Malhotra was not presently in a relationship with Sonya Rana as is being portrayed. The deceased had cut off all ties with Jay Malhotra. They were good friends. In the past few months, Jay was busy with his assignments at his parents' owned advertising firm and had not met Sonya for a long time. How can he be held responsible for Sonya's death? The last time the deceased met my client, she herself threw him out of her house. There is no motive to kill or abetment." Acharya's throat was parched after his little speech, and he reached for the glass of water.

The judge considered his argument for a moment and then looked down at the papers in his hands.

"Your honour, my client is not a flight risk and is innocent. I request bail be granted." Acharya looked hopeful and smug, which Nabar immediately disliked.

Sandhya and Rishabh waited anxiously. There was pin-drop silence in the courtroom. Rishabh knew chances were slim of Jay making it home today. He wrapped his hand around Sandhya's shoulder as she sobbed.

"After listening to arguments from both sides, bail is denied to Jay Malhotra."

A loud murmur arose in the courtroom, and Judge Nabar had to bang the gavel.

"Please maintain court decorum. I hereby order Jay Malhotra to be taken into police custody under abetment charges. He will remain in police custody till 20th July and hereby order the police to carry on with their investigations. I want a detailed report on the authentication of the letter produced in court today."

Judge Nabar gathered his robe and walked to the inner chambers, leaving chaos in his wake.

There were sounds of protests, chairs being scraped, media jostling to get a byte from Jay, capture his parents' shocked expression, Ramola's jubilant smile, Jay's tears, and Acharya's disappointment.

Jay was led to the waiting police van and whisked away from the courtroom before any journalist could reach him.

Sandhya was too shocked to react at the events that unfolded before them. The journalists crowded around them, shouting out questions and asking for a reaction.

Rishabh finally decided he would speak. "Jay is innocent. I have full faith in the Indian judiciary system. Truth will prevail."

"Is it true that your son was having an affair with Sonya and then left her? She was heartbroken and hence committed suicide, is this true?" one young girl questioned Sandhya, and the rest seconded her. Everyone seemed to be talking at the same time.

Sandhya looked at Rishabh, perturbed. He nodded for her to speak.

"It's not a crime to be in love. Jay and Sonya were good friends. They were busy with professional commitments. They just drifted apart," Rishabh held on to Sandhya's hand throughout. He was seeking comfort from his wife, calming his battered nerves.

"Excuse us… please," Rishabh led a distraught Sandhya to their waiting car. The thought that their son was driven away in a police van and here she was travelling in a Mercedes pained her hear—

As Jay walked through the prison corridors, a wave of fear washed over him. The walls seemed to close in on him, leaving him claustrophobic, and he broke into a sweat. Jay had a strong urge to turn and run. With great difficulty, he calmed himself.

Ins. Pawar collected Jay's personal belongings and put them in a box labelled with Jay's name. He then asked Jay to follow him to the assigned cell.

Pawar had been in the police service for the last 30 years. He had seen many criminals and escorted many of them to their cells.

Pawar had followed the news closely and believed in Jay's innocence. "This place is not meant for young lads like you."

Tears welled up in Jay's eyes.

"I pray to God you leave this place soon," Pawar murmured as he opened the cell door for Jay.

A nervous Jay stepped in. It was a tiny space with a single bed taking up the right-hand corner, a toilet bowl on the left side, and a tiny square hole in the wall served as a window to the world outside which had turned against him. Jay heard the metallic clang as the door shut, and he shuddered; the reality sunk in. He was in prison.

Jay paced up and down; restless as ever. The stink from the toilet bowl was unbearable, and the walls damp. The floor was cold like the metal bars keeping him in from the outside world. He could hear the rain pattering outside.

He sensed bile rise in his throat and threw up in the toilet bowl.

✳ ✳ ✳

Jay was brought to the interrogation room where ACP Arjun Deshmukh was already waiting. Arjun was young, in his late twenties, known for being a cool-headed and level-headed person. He was a cop who did not base his opinions on allegations but took a thoughtful and logical approach and then arrived at a conclusion. He believed in the theory that 'a criminal should not be spared, and an innocent should not be hanged'.

When Jay took his seat on the wooden chair, Arjun realised the lad had not slept a wink. Obviously, he was used to the comforts of luxuries his life provided him with. What he liked about Jay was that he did not resist or show any signs of non-cooperation. It seemed Jay was in a tearing hurry to get this thing over and done with.

Arjun stared at him for a while, as Jay looked at his hands and tried to steady the slight tremble that was setting in. His hair was in shambles and a stubble had grown on his chin since the day he was arrested. Arjun flicked open the file before him and went through the list of questions drawn up by his subordinate. Arjun raised his eyebrows in consternation, knowing very well he would cover the grounds on his own terms.

"Jay Malhotra… tell me something about yourself," Arjun knew this question would relax Jay. If he was guilty or if Arjun was plain lucky, it would throw him off guard. Who doesn't like to speak about themselves?

"My dad, Rishabh Malhotra, owns an advertising firm, and I work with him. My mom is a housewife," Jay nervously looked around, his heart racing.

"You are good-looking and can give any actor a tough competition. Any dreams of becoming an actor?" Arjun wanted to know if Jay was using Sonya's stardom for personal gains.

"Never…I am happy working in my dad's advertising firm." Jay took in a deep breath, trying to regain some kind of semblance to the curve ball life had thrown at him.

"Did you at any point use Sonya's star status to boost your career?" Arjun decided to use a direct approach. He wanted to shake things up a little. Here Jay looked up sharply, hurt obvious on his face.

"I mean, you run an advertising firm and… markets being so volatile… it doesn't hurt to know people in high circles. Correct me if I am wrong." Arjun wiped the sweat beads from his forehead. The rickety fan clocked its arms above.

"I would never use Sonya for something like this. That's so low and cheap," Jay looked at the fly that buzzed around his head and settled down on the circular mark left by a cup of tea or coffee.

"Hmmm… how close were you and Sonya? By close, I mean, were you both in an intimate relationship?"

"We were very close. We were in love and often spent time together," Jay stated matter-of-factly.

Arjun paused mid-way through his scribbling. "You were in love? So now you are no longer in love, or you were no longer in love before Sonya killed herself, or you ceased to be in love after Sonya died?"

Arjun knew you can't stop loving someone even after your loved one's death. Arjun still loved his father... even after the ordeal his father put him and his mother through. When God decides to give pain, he is not thinking of the measures but judging your tolerance level. Arjun had taken a leaf out of life's lesson.

Jay took a deep breath, hassled by the line of questioning. It looked like he did not want to answer the question, or he was avoiding giving an answer.

Arjun opened the file, a motion he went through thrice since he had placed it on the table and withdrew the letters from it. The first letter that he pushed towards Jay was addressed to Sonya.

Dear Sonya,

Missing you at every step of my life. Every day rises with a hope to see you, see your smile, see your sun-kissed hair and hear you whisper sweet nothings in my ears. I dream about us, dream about a life together. I want to protect you, see that no harm comes your way. Sonya, life without you is unimaginable. You taught me to live life, enjoy every moment.

I want to take you away from your worries, smooth the creases on your brow, your frowns ☹ ☹ and ups and downs. Let's do something wild that you love so much! ☺

Sonya, when life seems unbearable, think of me. Think of the time that we spent together, about our love and promises. I am sure they will bring a smile to your face.

I love you, Sonya, and I will always be there by your side when you need a friend and a soulmate.

Love you sweets.

Yours and only yours,

Jay.

Jay had only to glance through the letter once to know that it was written by him. He was still old school. Believed in writing letters instead of sending out text messages. His handwriting was something he had often prided himself on. He had been winning accolades for his handwriting since school, and his notebooks were a matter of pride for the school, to serve as an example of model handwriting for students.

Jay gave it a moment, held the letter in his hands, and nodded a yes, acknowledging the letter to be written by him.

"What worries were you talking about here?" Arjun looked into Jay's eyes.

"Jay … I am afraid this darkness will kill me. This evil in me is eating me alive, Jay. No one can help me." Sonya's words haunted him.

"That's none of your business," came as a sharp retort. Jay looked flustered.

"It's my business now, Mr. Jay Malhotra. Do not forget you are being questioned for your girlfriend's suicide."

"I do not understand what you want. Are you assuming that I am a criminal and questioning me, or is this how you question everyone… criminal or not?" It seemed more like a sarcastic comment than a question.

"Sonya was physically abused by our uncle when she was a child," Tania had revealed to a shocked Jay one day. *"Raking up the past is a torment for Di."*

"Vikram was the diabolical trapped within Sonya, and it was Vikram who finally killed her!" Jay clutched his head tightly and shut his eyes.

"Let the past be buried. Sonya is gone and with her, the evil."

Arjun did not answer but gave him a pointed look. Jay stared at his hands. He took a deep breath and looked up at Arjun, who was waiting for him to speak. Arjun was wary of getting emotionally involved.

"The worries mentioned in the letter meant trifling matters ... nothing serious." Jay's nonchalance led to doubts in Arjun's mind. He made a note to probe the question again. Who was Jay trying to protect? Sooner or later, he would speak. Prison life did not suit everybody, Arjun thought.

'Were you leading Sonya on to a path of self-destruction, unknown to you maybe? What happened between you two, that you both parted ways?'

"Something that I did not initiate. I loved Sonya. I failed her. I did not see it coming. I should have read the signs." The memories made him restless and not doing enough, mortified him.

"Did Sonya call to say she was going to US?" Arjun asked.

"Sonya was not in a condition to speak. She threw me out of her house and her life, locked herself in her room for a week, completely cut off from the outside world. I must have called Sonya like crazy. Then one day, Sonya called and said she was in New Jersey. They had left without informing anyone, not even me." Jay nodded his head in disbelief.

"Any idea why Sonya did not inform you about her trip to New Jersey?" Arjun asked, scribbling in his diary.

"As I told you, we had stopped meeting. It was Sonya who had stopped communicating with me. So, I had no idea when she left for the US. I knew Ramola aunty was taking her there for treatment but..." There was a sense of disconcert in Jay's words.

"Were you able to get in touch with Sonya then?" Arjun carefully made notes.

"After two months, I received a call from Sonya. She said she had been in psychiatric care for two months now and was feeling better but from the sound of it... she was a bit low." Jay now remembered how surprised he was to hear from her and happy too. Jay had decided he would tell Sonya he was tired of these cat-and-mouse games, and she should come to a decision regarding them both. But then he did not want to push her.

"Was she nervous?" Arjun was sitting on the edge of the chair, curious to know what exactly Sonya wanted from Jay, who now looked lost.

Jay spoke after a long pause. "She sounded tremendously disturbed. I asked her if Ramola aunty was with her, but she gave me some vague answers. She also said that she had this weird feeling that someone was watching her or following her every movement."

Arjun did not want to interrupt, so he let him speak. "I wanted to know if she had completed her treatment, why she was not coming back. Sonya said her mom had some urgent work and needed her signature on some papers, so they had to stay back. Something was wrong." Arjun was taking notes. He looked up puzzled.

"Why do you say that? Did she tell you what papers she signed? Arjun once again checked Sonya's file and came across her passport.

"I didn't know if she signed any papers. She didn't speak on that subject, and I didn't ask her again. I was worried for her. Sonya's speech was garbled... not clear. She was sobbing. I somehow managed to calm her down and assured her that I would call her every day, and I did call her every single day... but at times she answered, at times calls went unanswered," Jay trailed off.

"Coming back to Sonya's fears of being watched. Did she say who it was?"

Arjun noticed Jay thinking hard, genuinely trying to come up with an answer.

"Anything you can remember from your conversations with Sonya. It's pertinent to our investigation." Arjun tried to add pressure on Jay's memory. The lad was doing his best to remember. Finally, he nodded in negative, frustrated.

Arjun was still not happy with the way the investigation was progressing. Something told him there was a different angle to this whole Sonya suicide case. He closed the file and decided to call it a day.

* * *

It was a quaint Victorian-style bungalow, in far suburbs of Mumbai, with its porch opening out to the sound of waves lashing the shore. The steps leading up to the porch were covered by dry leaves. Within the confines of the walls grew roses of every colour. A circular pond stood in one corner where ducks had made it their home and birds quenched their thirst. Two brass lamps hung on either side of the porch, casting their warm yellow glow during the night. Nailed to the main door was a mask with long oval eyes, an elongated nose, and wide lips. It was red and white in colour, matching the brick wall outside. It was probably used to ward off evil. Metallic chimes of stars and moons hung on the door and chimed when the door opened.

Inside, the house was warm and grey. A quilt lay on the couch facing the television set in the living room, which was tuned to a news channel. Books lay strewn on the table along with empty coffee cups and half-eaten food. There was a piano kept against the wall, and above it on the shelf were used candles; their wax curled at their feet. The curtains were drawn together as if the occupant was weary of sunlight.

A woman sat on the chair with a sketchbook open before her. She was in her mid-fifties. Jay and Sonya's news was being played on the channel. The reporter was reporting the latest development, showing Jay being led to prison and an image of his parents sobbing. The woman's gaze was on the TV set, but her hands furiously sketched in the book before her. Her movements were brisk, and her gaze riveted to the news being broadcast. Soon she put down the pencil and, exhausted, lay with her head down. The reporter was drawing inferences from the trial and talking about Jay's bleak future.

The doorbell roused her from her drowsy state. She walked to the door, every moment an effort. As she opened the door, the moon and stars chimed, welcoming Nandini into the house.

"Hey, Maya… what's up?" Nandini chirped, following the woman to the living room. Her curls were in a mess after the auto ride. She weaved her fingers to untangle them. The scarlet top she wore with a cowl neck and blue denim hugged her petite frame.

"Nandini… thank God you are here. I just had a vision and…" Maya looked hassled.

"Calm down, Maya… that's okay… let me help you," Nandini tried to relax the older woman, led her to the couch, and fetched her a glass of water. She cajoled her into lying down while she prepared tea for them both.

Maya was what many would call a clairvoyant. A mystic with an ability to connect with souls who had passed. They all had a story to tell; they sought her help for a peaceful crossover. These conversations often left her exhausted, disturbing her aura.

Nandini offered Maya a steaming cup of tea and opened the packet of chocolate cookies she had brought with her. Nandini knew Maya needed a sugar boost, and cookies would do the trick.

Later, Nandini perused the fresh sketches drawn by Maya and came away amazed. This was not the first time the mystic in Maya had surprised her, but the results that she saw before her eyes perplexed her.

"OMG… Maya, this could be the breakthrough we were waiting for in the Sonya suicide case," Nandini's eyes became wide with excitement. It would speed up the investigation.

"Maya, did Jay's mother get in touch with you? I had left a note with your number with her the other day outside the court." Maya shook her head.

"On the day Jay was arrested, I had visions. I sensed Sonya in an ethereal form pointing towards Jay. She wants me to protect him. I decided to pay him a visit." Maya drew a deep breath.

"I wanted to warn Jay, but before I could do anything, the police took him away." Maya felt sorry for not having done anything for Jay.

Nandini listened in amazement. She once again flipped through the sketches. This was not the first time Nandini was hearing about Maya's encounter with spirits, but it still gave her goosebumps.

* * *

Arjun Deshmukh sat across from Nandini in the coffee shop where he had agreed to meet her. Nandini was his asset, and she felt the same about the cop. A crime reporter who always provided him with tips and clues to any incidents taking place in the city, but it was a give and take. Arjun too had to part with valuable information or give her a lead for her crime report. Today, what Nandini revealed to him was hard to digest.

"Are you nuts? This kind of evidence won't stand in court. I don't believe this, Nandini! How can an educated girl like you fall for this?" Arjun said, exasperated, as he shook his head at the sketches that Nandini had just handed him.

A fine line of worry dotted Nandini's forehead, which slowly spread to anger.

"You didn't even look at it! So, do you think I am wasting your time? Do you think all this is unreal? You do not believe in the afterlife, but does it mean it doesn't exist at all? I am not asking you to present them in court!" Nandini angrily stuffed the sketches in her bag and appeared flustered.

"Do you have any lead, Mr. Cop?" Nandini called Arjun 'Mr. Cop' when she lost her cool on him. She tilted her head, brows raised, hand on her waist as she posed the question to Arjun.

"Nandini, listen to me... all eyes are on this case. The world is keeping track of Jay's life through the media. What do you want me to do? Dish out these sketches? What do I tell them, huh? What do I tell the judge?" People around them started giving the two quizzical glances, and Arjun, embarrassed, lowered his voice.

"You don't have to prove anything to anyone. Maya has never failed me. I trust her." Nandini got up to leave.

"Nandini... please try to understand. It all sounds absurd," Arjun tried to stop her. He wanted to talk to someone badly. Sonya's case had him spending sleepless nights.

Nandini looked at Arjun and he realised how deeply he had hurt her, but he was helpless. However, he liked the girl and never had the courage to admit it. Arjun knew he could not take a chance with the Sonya-Jay case.

"The least you can do is follow this lead... please? Sonya did not die because of Jay. I have a strong feeling... Sonya's suicide case... there is something more to it than what meets the eye."

Having said this, Nandini left Arjun with a thought to chew on.

Arjun jerked out of his musings with sound of his cell ringing. It was Vishwas, his assistant.

"Sir, Sonya's mother is here at the police station. She wants to meet you." Vishwas sounded stressed.

This woman could be difficult to handle and must be giving his men a tough time, Arjun thought, remembering his meeting at Sonya's house.

"I'll be there in ten minutes, Vishwas," Arjun hurried out of the café. He rode to the police station all the time thinking about what Nandini had said.

What did the girl mean by 'there is something more to it than what meets the eye?' He had shared his thoughts with her? Arjun decided to visit the crime scene once again.

It had been a hell of a week since Jay's arrest. The boy was young and appeared to be innocent, and the girl who ended her life was vulnerable. She did not have to die.

There is something more to it than what meets the eye.

Was it true? Arjun shook his head in disbelief. He had started believing in Nandini's supernatural stories, which were unacceptable to him!

As Arjun entered the police station, he saw a flustered Vishwas pacing outside the cabin door.

"Vishwas, what's wrong?" Arjun asked, concerned, and the look of relief that passed through his subordinate's face did not go unnoticed.

"Sir, thank God you are here. I don't know what wrong I did today to deserve this. I even went to the Hanuman temple this morning as an everyday ritual but… no use I think." Vishwas seemed to be blabbering as he pointed towards Arjun's cabin.

Before Arjun could say anything, Sawant, a junior officer, butted in, "Praying to Hanumanji won't protect you from a woman's ire. Hanumanji is the God of bachelors, and you are a married man."

Arjun threw a stern look at Sawant, who quickly walked away. Generally, Arjun was never the strict disciplinarian, but today he could see Vishwas was genuinely disturbed and it became necessary to maintain the decorum of the police station … at times.

When Arjun entered his cabin, he found Ramola Rana flipping through a magazine. There were empty cups on the table with tell-tale signs of black coffee. Her designer handbag, which appeared expensive, was casually strewn across, as if this was not Arjun's cabin but her living room. Arjun, with great difficulty, controlled his temper and called for Sawant, who came running into the cabin. Ramola looked at him sideways and put on an act of nonchalance.

"Sawant, why haven't you cleaned my desk? What are these files doing here?" Arjun said a little sternly. Sawant started clearing the table and in a hurry, he picked up Ramola's handbag too. Ramola angrily flicked it from his hands.

"Sorry, madam… Arjun sir does not like his desk in a mess." Having finished clearing the table, Sawant left, closing the door behind him.

"Mr. Arjun Deshmukh, I have given you two more letters written by Sonya to nail Jay. It's a watertight case, and I hear he might be out on bail in the next hearing? This is ridiculous."

Ramola was a straightforward woman and could be mean too, and Arjun hated her guts for that.

"We are conducting an in-depth inquiry. The case cannot be tried based on letters. I need a motive. The law says we can't hang an innocent until proven guilty for the crime. I don't have to tell you that, Madam." Arjun wondered what was going on in this woman's mind. Why had she cancelled her US trip a day before Sonya's death?

"You mean to say you don't care about my deceased daughter. Her death is futile, that is what you are implying?" She looked at him squarely in his eyes. Her eyes were grey. Old age had not been kind on her. Wrinkles lined her skin from beneath her eyes, stretching to her jawline. She had freckles on her cheeks, and the fair complexion did nothing to hide the angry brown spots. However hard he may try; he could not find any similarities between the mother and daughter. But then how will he? Sonya was Ramola's stepdaughter!

Arjun was staring right through her, and this irked Ramola.

"Are you even listening to me? I am talking about my daughter and here you are daydreaming..."

Arjun turned his attention to Ramola, who had now taken to ranting.

"Madam, please control yourself. You can't come in here and accuse me of being careless or disinterested in Sonya Rana's case. I am doing my best."

Ramola seemed flustered at Arjun's retort, and she decided it was wise not to say more.

Ramola got up to leave. "Mr. Deshmukh, I hope you treat this case on an urgent basis. My daughter's soul won't rest in peace unless her murderer is punished," saying this, Ramola was about to storm out when she froze on the question posed by Arjun.

"Are you in touch with Meher Rana, or have you heard from her recently? Did Sonya meet her birth mother?"

Ramola turned to face him. She had composed herself. Piercing her lower lip, her eyes darting around nervously, Ramola approached his desk.

"That woman didn't mean anything to Sonya or to my family. I haven't met her in my entire lifetime, and Raghav hasn't spoken of her either. Now, if you please, can I leave?"

Arjun nodded in agreement. Ramola put on her sunglasses and walked out, banging the door behind her.

The mere mention of Meher had rattled Ramola. She was hiding something.

Arjun was toying with the paperweight on his desk as he contemplated Nandini's findings. He knew he could not ignore what Nandini was trying to tell him. Arjun decided to deal with that tricky part later. There was one person that he needed to meet up with.

When Arjun reached the doctor's clinic, the last patient for the evening was leaving. He was straight away summoned to the doctor's cabin.

Arjun sat across Dr. Kulkarni on the sprawling couch which was meant for his patients. He noticed there was a considerable gap between the doctor's chair and the couch.

"I don't like my patients to feel I am invading their space or being overbearing."

Arjun was startled, wondering if Dr. Kulkarni had read his mind.

Dr. Kulkarni had been briefed by his assistant about the reason for Arjun's visit. The doctor just stared ahead, and for a moment, Arjun felt it was a "reversal of roles". After what seemed like an eternity, he finally spoke.

"Sonya was an emotional wreck when she first came to see me. She was sitting right there," he pointed to where Arjun sat, "so young... beautiful but broken from within." The doctor paused.

"Who referred Sonya to you, doctor?" Arjun asked, nervously shifting a bit to his right.

"Their family physician, Dr. Desai, referred her to me. I have previously counselled some of the actors, and Dr. Desai knew I would be perfect for Sonya's case with the expertise required."

"Sonya's case? How serious was her case, doctor?" Arjun's thought process had begun.

"Sonya to an extent had bounced back, but somewhere deep down, I knew this condition of hers was temporary. It was all waiting to happen... all over again!" Dr. Kulkarni sighed as he removed his glasses, wiped them with a piece of cloth, and wore them back.

Arjun sensed the doctor knew more than he was letting on.

"Could you please elaborate? Any piece of information will help me in this case," Arjun said. As he said this, the doctor turned his gaze towards him.

"Her mental state was fragile. It was like a tip of an iceberg, ready to crumble. During the sessions, she sobbed uncontrollably, and the next moment broke into laughter. At times, she became hysterical. Sonya was a nervous wreck. I had prescribed her anti-depressants and sedatives to deal with her insomnia. She had a history of clinical depression caused by..." Dr. Kulkarni pondered whether he should let him in on the childhood incident that had haunted Sonya. He shrugged.

"By what, Doc...?" Arjun closed the gap between them in two strides and now stood before him.

"I don't know if I should be parting with personal information of my client who is deceased. If you insist but promise none of this is going out of this room," Dr. Kulkarni had a weary look on his face.

"I promise to keep whatever information you share between the two of us," Arjun waited, hoping for the answers he was seeking.

Dr. Kulkarni nodded. He walked to the file cabinets and, opening a drawer, took out a file with Sonya's name printed on it.

"What I am doing next is against my work ethic but here I make an exception. I was fond of Sonya. She was a sweet girl in a lot of pain. I tried my best, but I knew, after a point, my sessions were not helping her."

"Sonya's mind was a ticking bomb waiting to explode. Her pain was deep-rooted. Sonya, as a child, suffered sexual abuse by Vikram, Ramola Rana's brother," Arjun was shocked at this new piece of information.

"I am sure Ramola Rana must not have let you in on this. Sonya's father knew and to an extent Ramola too knew about this. No one protected her, except for her stepsister, Tania, and that broke her heart. Her loved ones' acquiescence left an ugly bruise on her being, more than the abuse." Dr. Kulkarni's voice became heavy with sorrow.

Arjun was numb with shock as he took Sonya's file. He opened it and came across a smiling face. Only when he could connect the dots of the previous history to Sonya's present smile did he realise the smile was fake, and there was so much sorrow and pain hidden beneath it.

The doctor looked at the watch and started packing his stuff.

"Doctor, what do you think about Jay Malhotra? I mean from Sonya's point of view. Did Sonya talk about Jay hurting her along with stuff she shared during sessions with you?" Arjun was anxious to get an answer from the doctor. His investigation depended on it.

"Sonya rarely mentioned Jay, as if he were her well-protected secret. In fact, I had noticed her smile at the mention of Jay." The doctor shook his head, sadness, and pain on his face.

"Officer, I think you should speak to Tania. The two sisters were close. She might be able to give insight about Sonya." Dr. Kulkarni's parting words stayed with Arjun as he left.

Arjun had found what he was looking for. He needed to meet up with Ramola and find out why she had maintained silence when Sonya was sexually abused by her brother. If the abuse was true, then wasn't Ramola also responsible for Sonya's death? A question he asked himself a thousand times after he left the clinic. He reminded himself to speak with Gaurav too.

Sandhya herself was searching for answers to these very questions that haunted her since Sonya's death. Only if she had spoken to Sonya one last time. This was a fortnight before Sonya ended her life. Sandhya had this strange feeling that she should speak with Sonya. However hard she tried to shake it off her mind, it refused to go. Would Sonya talk to her if she called? Did she still think Jay used her to get lucrative projects? Then Sandhya had doubts but today she regretted not taking that chance and talking to the young girl.

Sonya was in love with Jay. What puzzled Sandhya was why she pushed Jay away when he expressed his love for her?

Sandhya was now standing outside Ramola's apartment. Ramola had refused to speak with her. It was Gaurav who answered her calls. Unable to tolerate Ramola's indifferent attitude towards Jay, Sandhya had made up her mind to personally pay her a visit.

"Sandhya, there is nothing to talk about now, is there?" Ramola said as soon as she saw Sandhya at her doorstep.

"I am sorry for your loss, but you should know my son has nothing to do with it. Jay has always tried to help Sonya in her times of distress." Sandhya felt emotions building within her. She was deeply pained by Sonya's going away.

"Jay refused to meet Sonya, turned her away when she needed him," Ramola snapped angrily.

Sandhya remembered Sonya coming over, asking for Jay. She seemed disturbed and anxious as well.

"Jay was not in town when Sonya came looking for him. Ramola, you knew how close both kids were. You were aware of Sonya's state of mind. She was not keeping well for a long time now. Then how can you say that Jay is responsible for what happened to Sonya? Why didn't you tell the police about Sonya's mental condition?" Sandhya was now losing her patience. She realised Ramola was not ready to budge from her stand.

"How dare you bring Sonya's mental condition into play to save your son? Jay used Sonya's name to secure contracts for your advertising firm many times. I have heard Sonya speak up for him. Jay even persuaded her to model for your client, and was paid pittance. Sonya never cared about money; she cared about relationships. Jay took advantage of her vulnerability," Ramola was screaming now.

Sandhya also lost her temper. After all, it was a matter of her son's life.

"Ramola, you were aware of Sonya's psychological condition. What she was going through was no less than that of a mentally ill person!" Sandhya could not believe she had said that.

"How dare you call my daughter mentally ill? If she were, then why was Jay still sticking by her? I am sure he had a hidden agenda of his own," Ramola trembled with anger.

Both women did not realise that Tania was watching them from the door to her room. Tania so much wanted to speak up for her sister but feared Ramola.

"Sonya's letters prove that she held Jay responsible for her suicide. Why would Sonya lie when she was fond of Jay? He did not convince Sonya to go to US for treatment. He wanted her here for his own selfish reasons." Ramola remembered her conversation with Jay that evening when she had asked for his help. Sonya's condition had worsened after Jay left.

"You are getting this all wrong, Ramola. My son is innocent. He was in love with Sonya," Sandhya mumbled, devastated, seeing the discussion not going anywhere. Ramola walked out of the room.

A moment later, Sandhya felt a hand on her shoulder. She was surprised to see it was Tania.

"Aunty, I believe you," Tania offered her a glass of water. Sandhya accepted it with trembling hands.

"Tania, you knew Sonya, you knew Jay. He would never intentionally hurt Sonya!" Sandhya was trying hard to convince Tania about Jay's innocence.

"Jay and Sonya Di were in love. Jay had proposed marriage to Di, and she refused." This was news to Sandhya.

"Jay did ask for references from Di as mom says, but Di did not seem to mind it. Jay cared about her a lot."

"Will you tell this to the police? It will help get bail for Jay," Sandhya asked hopefully.

"Aunty, as of now, I can't go against mom. She is still in shock and in denial," Sandhya was surprised at Tania's words.

"Don't worry, I will try to convince mom, make her understand Jay's innocence. Till then, please don't try to get in touch with mom." Tania went away as Sandhya, baffled, looked on.

Should she put her faith in Tania? Did she just promise to help her and cooperate with her? What was going on in Tania's mind? Sandhya left with lots of questions and no answers she had come in search of!

✷ ✷ ✷

Jay was moved to a larger cell. As he did his usual push-ups, his mind was never far from Sonya. He remembered her every waking moment. He had been in love with her. It was she who rudely pushed him away one day and refused to take his calls. "I shouldn't have given up on her," thought Jay.

The sound of his cell door clanging open jerked him out of his musings. He did not like the intrusion as he found solace with Sonya in his thoughts.

A young, lean fellow, around eighteen years of age was roughly pushed into his cell by the policeman, and the door was once again locked. The boy was dressed in unkempt clothes and looked like some wrangle from the roadside. His ego looked crushed for being pushed and heckled by the policeman. He looked at Jay and tried to pull himself together. Suddenly, he recognised Jay.

"*Aaila*...you are Sonya ka item? Gullu...how are you?" His eyes widened with amazement, and mouth agape, he extended his hand. Jay shook hands with the boy who immediately sat down next to him.

"So, this is what people referred to him as!" The thought amused him.

"I remember seeing you and Sonya." He appeared street-smart.

"You were at the bandstand buying ice cream," Gullu said excitedly.

Jay nodded, remembering their visit to bandstand for ice-cream. They would sit in the car eating ice-cream and later they would watch the sun set with the waves crashing onto the rocks. Gullu's voice brought Jay to the present.

"Didi was kind to me. I was begging at the signal when I saw her. Police brought me in for begging. My sister also begs but at a different signal. Ohh…oh, I forget what I was saying. Coming back to Sonya didi…I thought she would give me money. But she gave me her gold ring instead."

That was Sonya, kind and benevolent. Jay was overwhelmed by the memory Gully shared with him.

"I hid the ring from my father, who drinks and beats us up. Can I tell you one thing?" Gullu didn't wait for Jay to answer. "She looked sadly at you. I don't believe you killed her."

Jay turned, facing the wall, sobbing. He could hear Gullu whistling a song from Sonya's movie and doing a hook step from the song.

The next morning, as Jay queued for a bath, he heard commotion from one of the bathrooms. At first, he decided to ignore it as his lawyer had asked him to stay out of fights, but he heard a familiar voice crying out in pain, "Don't hit me … bhaiyya … please… help me."

Jay made his way through the crowd of inmates and now stood outside the tiny cubicle which served as the bathroom. There was only a thin partition of a towel between them. The cries had increased, and by now Jay was sure it was his cellmate, Gullu.

"Let me go... I did not steal your bar of soap... bhaiyya... help me... aaahhh..." His cries were followed by slaps.

Jay pulled aside the curtain and saw a huge man beating Gullu, who was bleeding through his nose and mouth. When Jay reminisced later about the rash step he took, he still could not understand what came over him then. Only one thought had filled up his mind: to protect Gullu. Jay wound his arm around the brute's neck and pulled him away from Gullu and out into the open. Next, he shot a hard punch to his face and sent the man reeling to the ground.

The time spent in the gym had come in handy. Jay knotted his fist, pumped his muscles, his nostrils flared in anger as he readied for another punch. The rage and frustration of being wronged for a crime he had not committed, all bottled up until now, threatened to explode.

"How dare you?" Jay growled, his eyes filled with anger, his entire body trembling, eager to punch the man's face. The man was taken by surprise at the sudden assault and now cowered under Jay's angry presence.

Suddenly, the man lunged for Jay's legs, and Jay was about to kick him when the man started begging for mercy.

"I am sorry... please forgive me. I had no idea he was under your protection." The man had a soft voice unlike his rippling muscles and huge build. Jay was taken aback for a moment.

Jay reeling with anger; his stance remained unchanged. Gullu saw some police officers approaching from afar and tugged at Jay's arm.

"Bhaiyya … bhaiyya … let's go." He nodded his head in the direction of the approaching police. Jay took a deep breath, pulled the man to his feet and, staring hard at him, whispered in his face,

"Next time I see you hitting anybody... you are a goner," Jay knotted his fist, and one could hear the crunch of bones. The man beat a hasty retreat. When the police arrived on the scene, everyone behaved as if nothing had happened.

A couple of days later, one morning, as usual, Jay was doing push-ups in the open space outside his cell when he saw Gullu, walking towards him with a glass balanced carefully in his hands.

Gullu's bruises were healing now, and the swelling had gone down too. When the doctor asked Gullu if he was involved in any fight, Gullu said he slipped in the bathroom. The doctor nodded his head, understanding what must have transpired for those wounds to appear. He had come across many cases of "slipping in the bathroom" during his stint as a prison doctor.

"Jay bhaiyya… I brought hot milk for you." Then, he cast a wary glance around for eavesdroppers, if any, and whispered in a low voice, "Dry-fruit mixture has been added to it. Of course, I had to request it, but when I told the guy in the kitchen, I wanted it for the hero in barrack number seven, he generously added an extra spoon. Drink it… it's good for you." Gullu was pleased with himself for being of some use.

Jay patted his head and took the glass from the boy. He drank the milk and, true to what he said, it did contain a generous dollop of dried fruit mixture. The incident outside the bathroom had given him an ardent and loyal follower.

"Bhaiyya, I am going home," Gullu held Jay's hand. "I will ask maa to pray to Maa Bhavani for you. She will keep you safe."

Jay shook hands with Gullu.

"I will see you outside…soon. I am sure." Gullu smiled before turning to leave.

The cell doors opened, and Gullu walked out humming a tune from one of Sonya's movies. Jay watched as the young boy went away with the cop.

Arjun opened the door that led to the balcony in Sonya's room. The swing creaked as Arjun gave a gentle tug. He could see the dried patches of blood on the floor, and some on the edges of the swing.

Arjun stood there for a while, visualising what could have taken place that fateful night. To his surprise, the images that came to his mind bespoke a different story altogether.

Arjun was now an eight-year-old, hiding behind his mother's pallu, confused and shocked at the horrific events unfolding before him. From where he stood, he could see the thumbs of his father's feet and hands, tied together as was the ritual. His father had explained to him its significance once. After a person dies, his soul leaves the body and wanders around. His body is vulnerable to any wandering soul. Hence, the thumbs are tied to protect the body.

Little Arjun looked around and heard people murmuring in low voices about how the head was separated from the torso and had to be stitched together for the funeral. Arjun still shuddered at the images in his head. Sonya's suicide had evoked images from his childhood that were buried deep down in his memories.

Arjun had spoken to Dr. Kulkarni and had got a general idea about Sonya's state of mind. Sonya was depressed and emotionally unstable, but she was deeply in love with Jay. Was Jay in love with Sonya? If Jay and Sonya were in love with each other, then why did Sonya leave a letter blaming Jay for her death? What were the worries Jay was talking about in his letter to Sonya, and why did he talk about life becoming unbearable for Sonya?

Jay's interrogation had led him to believe that Jay and Sonya shared an intimate relationship, and Jay did not deny it at any point. He too seemed to be in shock at the extreme step taken by Sonya. Here, Arjun did not want to be judgemental or partial; hence, he was asking these questions to himself.

Arjun now stood in Sonya's bedroom. He took in the wardrobe and decided to search it. He was about to wear gloves when a window, at the far end of the room, flew open, and the curtains fluttered madly in the breeze. Sonya's picture frame fell to the floor. Arjun pulled the window shut and picked up the frame. Sonya was smiling, looking directly into the camera. Behind her, Arjun could see mountains, fog, and a deep valley. Her stance was that of a person who was on a dangerous adventure.

Death was always on her mind, thought Arjun as he replaced the photo frame on the side table.

Now what puzzled him was, despite knowing her daughter's state of mind, Ramola was pinning Sonya's death on Jay. Why? What did she aim to achieve by doing that? The tox report showed alcohol and traces of LSD in

Sonya's blood. Just then, he heard a buzzing sound. It came from behind the curtain. Arjun cautiously approached the window and parted the curtains. It was a dragonfly. Arjun sighed and opened the window to let it out. Suddenly, a thought struck him. He opened Sonya's file and read the tox report and the blood work. The doctor had mentioned that LSD was in the form of capsules, which went by the name 'Dragonflies' in the drug market. Who was supplying drugs to Sonya? Was it Jay? Or was it someone who wanted her dead?

Arjun somehow could not shake the feeling that Sonya's death was a complicated suicide. If Sonya was doing drugs, what had Ramola done to help her?

Arjun decided it was time to meet Ramola Rana. The woman needed to answer some questions.

As he was about to leave, Arjun heard footsteps approaching the apartment and halt outside the door. He waited for a moment and then opened the door and was surprised to find Nandini, hand mid-air, ready to knock.

"I am sorry to intrude like this. When I couldn't get through to your cell, I called your office and Inspector Vishwas directed me here."

Arjun had not spoken a single word in their twenty-minute ride to her house, and Nandini assumed he was angry. He still had that tight-lipped look on his face.

"I know it's a crime scene and I shouldn't be there. Sorry…" Nandini understood she had put Arjun in a fix. He grunted in reply.

Nandini looked at him, wondering if she should invite him in. She looked at Arjun, who was about to start his bike.

"Want to join me for a cup of coffee… um… my place?"

Nandini waited, anticipating a no. Would he take her up on her offer?

"Sure… are you okay with that?" he asked.

"Welcome!" That was quick, thought Nandini, smiling to herself, leading the way. Arjun followed with a wry smile on his face.

Later, at Nandini's place, as she got busy in the kitchen making coffee, Arjun stood in the hall admiring the various trophies and certificates she had received as an athlete.

"Those are from my school and college days. Though I don't run anymore," Nandini said, handing the cup to Arjun, who looked quizzical; her statement warranted details.

"This happened when I was back home in Darjeeling. My brother was teaching me to ride his bike and I skidded on the very first day of my training. I fractured my leg, and that was the end of my racing and riding bikes." Nandini pursed her lips in a smile, raising her brows, an expression of someone who had resigned herself to her fate.

"You sure do have a penchant for adventure, don't you?" Arjun remarked and turned his attention to the other photographs.

"Why did she feel that she was probed and analysed whenever he looked at her?" Nandini tapped her feet nervously, thinking where this was all heading. This was the first time she had a visitor at home. Nandini had friends from the workplace but none whom she invited over or socialised with.

Arjun was looking at a photograph of an elderly couple. Nandini bore a striking resemblance to the lady. "It must be her parents," thought Arjun. As he turned to look at Nandini, he found she was staring at him.

The connection between them was palpable. Arjun pulled her towards him, his arm going across her waist. The feel of her body against his, the softness of her skin as he rubbed his thumb against her cheek, her eyelashes drooping as his other hand rested on the small of her back. He could feel tension rise within him. Arjun avoided meeting her gaze as he knew he would be lost and then nothing would remain in his hands.

He felt Nandini's finger brush his cheek, and he did what he was warning himself against. Arjun gazed deeply into her eyes as he cupped her chin, raising it towards him and planted a kiss on her lips. At first, it was a hesitant kiss, but then he felt Nandini moving against him, reciprocating to his advances, and the kisses became more sensual and deeper. Arjun's hands started roaming freely on Nandini's body, exploring every curve. His tongue flicked around her delicate neck as he left trails of kisses on her shoulder. Nandini moaned in delight, clutching his arms tightly, for the sheer pleasure would have knocked her off her feet. The buttons on her cotton shirt popped open, and he slid it off her shoulders, hungrily kissing her luscious lips. Next, he unhooked her bra. His touch on her bare skin was electric as he cupped her breasts and kissed them, sucking and at the same time looking into her desire-filled eyes.

Soon their clothes lay in a heap on the floor as Arjun pushed her down on the couch, pressing his hardness against her. His hands now cupped her breasts, slowly kneading them in circular motions. Next, he drew erotic circles around her belly button, sending her brain into a tizzy. Nandini had no idea her body was capable of so many sensations as she felt them surge through her, all together, tingling her nerves to the core. Arjun's touch set her body on fire and awakened desires her body was alien to.

Arjun looked at Nandini once, to know if she wanted to take it further. He could see desire in her eyes, her lips parted and quivered, and she dug her fingers into his arms. Her brandy eyes did turn smoky when aroused, Arjun smiled. He could see questions on Nandini's face but only for a moment.

"Nandini, I want you now… but if you want me to stop…" Arjun did not want to take advantage of Nandini's vulnerability.

"Arjun… please… don't stop," Nandini urged, wrapping her arms around his neck as he bent down to kiss her. His name on her lips sounded sensual to his ears. As he plunged inside her, Nandini felt a sharp pain and gasped.

Arjun stopped and looked at her in bewilderment. "You did not tell me you were a virgin…"

"I am glad I saved it for the best," Nandini smiled, pulling him close. Arjun plunged deeper, trying to be as gentle as possible so as not to hurt her.

Nandini groaned, a heady mix of pain and pleasure. Every thrust took her to heights of ecstasy she had never experienced before. Arjun gazed deeply into her eyes, losing himself in the depth of them. He shuddered, emptying himself in her.

Sated, they both lay in bed, exhausted, and spent. Nandini was the first to awaken. She got dressed and gently tapped Arjun's shoulder, who seemed to have drifted away into a peaceful sleep. She had noticed a smile appear and fade on his lips.

Arjun roused and took a deep breath. He pulled Nandini into his arms, who initially protested but later gave in as Arjun nuzzled her neck, kissing her. Nandini once again felt her body temperature soar.

"Stop it... please... not now," Nandini tried to push him away, but Arjun held her beneath him, hands pinned to the bed.

"So, there is a next time," he asked, kissing her passionately.

"You are wicked, Mr. Arjun Deshmukh," Nandini said, squirming to free herself. Arjun let her go. He stared at her across the room as he got dressed.

Nandini wondered if it was the right time to broach Maya's subject. She was now standing close to him. "Why don't you meet Maya once? I am sure you will find a way to deal with the turmoil that's going on in your head," Nandini said, buttoning his shirt, looking into his eyes.

Arjun held her hand and stared at her. Was he so vulnerable? Did he wear his sorrow on his sleeves? Arjun smiled at Nandini. "Oh… so you have turned into a face reader!"

Nandini looked at him quizzically as Arjun placed a kiss on her palm.

"Don't bother your pretty head over me. Come, let me drop you at your office." Arjun kissed her on the cheek.

✳ ✳ ✳

Police Commissioner Chandra Sahay took to playing snooker at the club to curb his loneliness and stress. Giving him company was a chilled Corona. It was the only option to drive away the sweltering heat of the island city.

Despite the air conditioning, sweat poured down his forehead as he waited for his turn to 'pot' the ball. Then he saw Arjun walk towards him, and a smile lit up his cherubic face.

Sahay had a fair complexion, and his cheeks were the colour of tomatoes, especially when he was happy about something or either stressed and sweating. He was glad to see Arjun.

CP Sahay was in his late fifties, balding and on the heavier side. His colleagues snickered when he passed them in the office corridors, commenting that "Sahay waddled like a duck instead of walking." His big butt bore the brunt of many jokes that did the rounds of the office. Sahay was immune to them all as he loved his staff, and they showed their affection by sharing their homemade food with him.

Sahay had not married or at least marriage was never on the cards as he put it. He led a solitary life with his Labrador Zach for company. Sahay had taken Arjun under his wing since the young lad had joined the police force. Sahay had known Arjun's father since they served under the Special Encounter Wing of the Police department, which did not exist on paper.

It was said, Sahay knew the reason why Arjun's father took such an extreme step, but he was protecting his colleague. Arjun never asked, as he knew Sahay would take his own sweet time to reveal the dark secrets that lay hidden in the depths of his mind.

"So, Arjun, it is high time you briefed me about the case." It was Sahay's break as the other elderly gentleman got ready to 'pot' the balls.

Sahay offered a bottle of Corona to Arjun, and the two walked to the veranda overlooking the lake. Neither of them talked, basking in solitude that the time offered. It was a ritual every Friday evening that both cops followed, off-duty, for the last 10 years, the exception being if either of them was out of town.

A few moments later, Sahay turned to Arjun and remarked, "Arjun, this city has changed a lot. I have seen it move from better to worse." He sighed.

"Did you notice the gap between the land and the sea shrinking? It's a warning sign. Humans are moving too fast... too fast."

"We are always in a tearing hurry, aren't we?" Arjun replied as the iciness of the drink percolated his senses, calming his nerves.

Sahay took a swig from the bottle and looked forlornly at the setting sun. His expression was that of a person who had given up all hope.

"People who opt to die do not for a moment think about their loved ones! Man has become so selfish. He has entered into an omnipresent race with God..." Arjun rubbed his lower lip with his right thumb, a trait he had picked up from his father when lost deep in thought.

Sahay gave him a grim look.

"By the way, what's happening with Sonya's suicide case? Any progress?"

"I am running into obstacles. Ramola has built these huge walls between us."

"You think someone killed Sonya and made it look like a suicide?" Sahay found this new angle interesting.

"It's a possibility which I am not willing to look over," Arjun said with enough fervour for Sahay to look surprised.

"I don't think you should handle Sonya's suicide case. I will transfer the case to some other officer," Sahay said after a long pause.

"You think my tumultuous past will influence my line of thinking? You know me better than that," Arjun reached for the papers in his briefcase and came back to where the senior cop stood contemplating his next move. He waved the papers before Sahay to drive home his point.

"I am on the verge of making a breakthrough in this case. After interrogating Jay and inquiring around the people Sonya socialised with, I think this case is not what we think it is… definitely not a simple suicide case. There are a lot of secrets to be unearthed."

"Arjun, you are opening a Pandora's Box… be careful." Arjun knew these words of wisdom stemmed from years of experience and expertise.

Sahay patted the young cop on his shoulder as he went through the papers. He handed them to Arjun with a grim look on his face.

"Many a times, answers lie in a person's past. Dig deeper and you will find the hidden truth."

"You think you can trust me? I am not giving up on this case. Maybe in this quest lie answers to my past too." Arjun winked, smiled, and walked away confident he was moving in the right direction.

It's a war raging inside a human head. The number of thoughts, feelings, emotions that are processed inside is not less than a battlefield. Arjun stood on the overhead railway bridge as people passed him unmindful of his presence. For them, he was one of the crowds, a non-entity just like them. They brushed past him, like perfect strangers offering him the solace of communicating with himself, respecting his privacy. Below, he could see trains zipping through the station, people alighting in hordes, pushing, jostling to get in. Body to body, thoughts to thoughts, and soul to soul, yet each one unique! Everybody is in a hurry, thought Arjun.

Arjun tries hard not to look at the tracks but instead seek out happy faces. He reckoned they could be counted on fingertips. Time and again his gaze wanders to the tracks. They were like a maze, interloping mass of metal, tempting, beckoning him. Unknown to him, he was drawn towards them, hypnotised. The tracks merges into one big track and suddenly it leapt towards Arjun, who, shocked by the sudden onslaught, staggers back.

Arjun is pushed into the throngs of people who look like an amalgamation of mass. They stick to Arjun's body, leaving their imprints on him. He can now hear their thoughts, their whispers, and their whimpering. Arjun fights them off. He wants to get away as far as possible. Arjun sees an opening and runs towards it. His feet feel like lead but he drags himself away from the crowd. He is carrying the weight of the tracks home.

When Arjun reaches home, he finds his goldfish swimming in the round glass bowl, oblivious to the chaos reigning outside. Is the fish happy? There is no way of knowing. The fish has not seen an ocean or, for that matter, a lake. His movements are restricted to the glass bowl as he shimmers in the water like a beacon of hope. Arjun sighs, feeding Goldie his dinner, tapping on the glass, trying to draw the fish's attention, but Goldie moves away. A mute partner to happenings outside his aquatic world, mused Arjun.

The frosty beer looked inviting after the turmoil in Arjun's mind. He retrieved it from the refrigerator and flopped down on the couch which had seen better days. He pulled the cushions towards him for comfort. The covers had faded with time, he noticed grimly.

Arjun had just settled in with his beer when he felt unease creeping up. He took a deep breath and stood up.

Suddenly, he felt his chest constrict and his breath stuck in his throat. The room shrunk, the walls getting closer and closer. Arjun remembered the breathing technique his shrink had taught him. Inhale till the count of four, hold till the count of four and exhale till the count of four. Eventually, he realised his mind had come back from whichever dark place it had been to.

Bile rose in his throat as he dashed to the sink and emptied his guts out. As he vomited, he felt an outside force was wrenching his intestines, twisting his tongue, forcing out the yellow acidic bile from his stomach. Arjun was amazed at the capacity of his stomach to churn out the acidic liquid. Does this acid reach the brain and make you act weird? Is that why people end up killing themselves? Does the chemical react with the brain and the heart, rendering it numb, giving birth to suicidal thoughts? It is the gut who is the culprit here. Everything starts from the gut, he deduced.

Arjun had just experienced the burning sensation through his stomach, to his throat, scalding his tongue. A wild thought came to his mind. He rushed to the terrace.

Arjun looked down from the 20th floor. From above, he saw a miniature world zipping by. A cold shiver passed through him. The wind blew in strong gusts, pushing him back. A lump arose in his throat. Arjun closed his eyes for a moment, and he saw tiny lights burst before him. From where had his dad gathered the strength to jump before a speeding train? How had Sonya surrendered to death?

The night turned dark, like the questions that raced in his mind. Suddenly, he felt calm wash over him; the wind had stilled. Arjun opened his eyes and knew what it felt like not wanting to die. For those whom the meaning of existence ceases, an end to the quest of the unknown, hope is no more, and desolation sets in are reasons people commit suicide. They are already dead before they embark on their last journey, Arjun thought. The night seemed colder than before. Arjun gingerly retraced his steps, pondering if he had got the answers he was looking for.

*** * ***

Jay sat in the interrogation room, seemingly dejected and nervous. Arjun observed him from the glass partition in the next room. Today, Jay was drumming his fingers on the table. It could mean two things; either he was getting impatient or would part with some information. Arjun was confident Jay knew more than he was letting on.

Jay looked up as the senior cop entered but was surprised to see that today he took the chair at the back of the room. A young cop entered after him and took the chair. He opened the file and started asking him questions directly. Jay noticed he was all business-like and not at all like Arjun, who seemed humane and even sympathised with him at a certain point.

"Mr. Jay Malhotra, when was the last time you met Sonya?" the cop asked coldly.

Arjun looked at Inspector Vishwas and knew he would play the "bad cop" to perfection. Vishwas always wanted to be an actor, but it was his father's wish that he joins the police force and serve society. Nonetheless, Vishwas was happy working with Arjun as he had learned a lot from him.

Jay took a deep breath and, in what seemed like a pause, replied, "the last time I met Sonya was two months before her..." Jay shuffled in the hard chair, swiped sweat off his nose; it was obvious he was disturbed, "the day she ended her life."

"Or you aided her to end her life..." Vishwas's statement was met with bitter scorn from Jay.

"I never did such a thing... never," Jay pressed on the last word "never" as if it meant life for him.

"Don't you think you pushed Sonya towards her death?" Vishwas was staring hard at Jay, pointing an accusatory finger at him.

"No ... No ... you may say what you may, but Sonya did not die because of me," Jay retorted angrily, flaring his nostrils. There was just a hint of tears in his eyes. He banged his fist on the table until it wobbled.

"We want to know why? We know you have the answers, but you are keeping something from us…" Vishwas prodded as Arjun looked on.

There comes a breaking point in a person's life, and Arjun could see Jay on the brink of it. His days in prison had taken a toll on his health and mind.

"Tell us about your last meeting with Sonya," Vishwas shuffled the papers from his file and waited for Jay to answer, all the while glancing at the papers in his hands.

"Don't you want to get out of this rut and move on in life?" Arjun asked from where he sat, in semi-darkness.

"You think I am having a good time locked up in jail! You don't know what it is to see your parents die, everyday bit by bit," Jay strained his neck in the direction of Arjun's voice, his nerves taut with tension.

"I loved Sonya, but a part of me will never forgive her for what she has done to me," Jay said with as much acrimony as he could muster.

Arjun winced at his outrage. He had not seen his mother die bit by bit but had seen her give up on life the day his father committed suicide.

Vishwas glanced over at Arjun, who immediately masked his feelings. He turned to Jay. "Why don't you tell us what you know and get it over with?"

Jay looked away from them both, towards the flickering light bulb, the rickety fan. He took in the cobwebs in the corners of the wall and then turned his gaze on the two cops. At least he was getting a chance to tell his side of the story and prove his innocence.

Barely a week had passed since he came to the prison. His chances of getting bail depended on what he revealed to the cops. It was time to tell everything that he knew about Sonya's past. It was not going to make a difference to Sonya now. With her, everything had died.

"My last meeting with Sonya was when she came to my office. I was in a meeting and hence had missed her calls. I heard a commotion outside my conference room. When the door opened, I could not believe my eyes. There she was standing all sloshed up, bottle in her hand, waving away my staff who tried to stop her. To avoid further scene, I led her to my cabin."

"This was after she came back from abroad, from the psychiatric care?" Arjun asked from the shadows.

Jay nodded in his direction. "Much later. She pushed me away, saying she was going to US again, taking a break. For a few moments, I just stared at her, puzzled. In our last meeting, Sonya had made it clear she didn't want to see me and now here she was, in my office, creating a ruckus. I thought she must have already left for US. Just when I was coming to terms with the break-up, she would reappear," Jay was staring listlessly at his fingers.

"So now Sonya had turned into a problem, had she?" Vishwas immediately caught on his vulnerable moment.

Jay looked up sharply at this question.

"Don't conjure imaginary stories. Sonya's inconsistent behaviour regarding us did affect me, but that doesn't mean I pushed her to her death."

Vishwas tapped his fingers on the table impatiently. "What did you do then?"

Jay wiped the sweat off his brow and began to speak again.

"I dropped her home then. She appeared disoriented. I did not want to leave her alone, so I called Ramola aunty as Sonya said, Ramola and Tania were staying in their other house, nearby." Jay remembered the night before Sonya's suicide.

"Why weren't they staying together? What did Ramola Rana have to say about this?" Arjun now walked up to Jay as he saw the conversation leading somewhere.

"I asked Sonya, but she was not in a condition to answer. Ramola aunty said she was busy getting things arranged. She sounded indifferent, angry." Jay remembered the exact tone Ramola had spoken in.

What possibly could have been more urgent than the well-being of her daughter? What had Sonya done to anger Ramola? Arjun wondered, twirling the pencil between his fingers.

"I called Tania, but Ramola aunty snatched the phone and warned me not to call again. She said something like…'teaching Sonya a lesson..'" Jay took a deep breath to control his tears.

Arjun walked over to where Jay was sitting. He offered Jay a glass of water which he accepted but didn't drink.

"Why didn't you wait with her?" Arjun could feel his jaw muscles getting taut. It happened when he was stressed.

"Sonya, shut the door on my face." Jay wondered if he should have stayed.

"If I had stayed back, would she be alive today?" The question was not meant specifically for anyone. Jay ran his fingers through his hair, clutching his forehead.

Arjun made a note to question Ramola about Jay's phone call to her.

"You want to tell us what happened between you and Sonya in your cabin? Presumably, that was your last meeting in person with Sonya, am I right?" Arjun had now pulled his chair much closer to Jay. He did not want to miss out on anything.

Whatever Jay was going to tell them could lead them to vital clues about Sonya's suicide. Something indeed did not smell right!

✳ ✳ ✳

Ramola Rana was still in mourning. It was barely a week since her daughter's death. Today, she seemed a little disturbed. She kept staring at her daughter's framed picture adorned with flowers and incense sticks. Though Sonya often laughed and smiled, the spark in her eyes had vanished long ago.

Ramola wondered if all her hopes and dreams had died with Sonya. Financially, she was well off. Sonya's earnings were neatly invested in her own name. Her husband had died a rich man. Tania had earned a master's in management. It was time to focus on Tania.

"I just hope the letters provide the police with all the proof they need to nail Jay. The police will then hopefully stop digging into Sonya's past." Ramola shivered at the thought of her reputation being at stake.

Ramola nervously chewed on her nails; the nerve on her forehead twitched. Tania was observing her mother closely. She knew some wicked thought must have passed through her mind.

Ramola noticed Tania watching her and then turning away. "Tania, you are well aware of the situation we are in right now. Please don't make things difficult for me," Ramola pleaded. "I want you to put your degree to some use. I had plans for both of you and see what happened…" She flung her hands in the air in despair at the turn of events.

"For I know the plans I have for you," declares the LORD, "plans to prosper you and not to harm you, plans to give you hope and a future."

Tania did not react to her mom's outburst.

Tania yawned, disinterest evident as she got up and reached for the bottle of coke. Ramola looked at her with a questioning glance.

"I have been meaning to ask you something, since the day you got back from the States," Ramola removed her glasses and looked directly at her daughter who had now paused mid-way, bottle inches away from her lips.

"What's this fascination with soft drinks?" Ramola's question didn't seem to have any effect on Tania, who shrugged, and without a word went to her room. Ramola kept calling out to her daughter, but she turned a deaf ear, banging her bedroom door on Ramola's face. Ramola was taken aback.

Ramola realised she had neglected Tania in the past few months. It was high time they had one of the mother-daughter chats.

Tania, indifferent to her mom's outburst, added Vodka to the bottle of Coke and carried it to the bed. Her mom had no idea Tania had taken to drinking and using drugs. That was one of the reasons Tania kept to herself. When under the influence of drugs, Tania was able to block out the constant fights between her parents, Ramola's nagging, and Vikram abusing Sonya going unnoticed and ignored, and Sonya's pain, her tears.

Despite having a sister, she was not allowed to interact with Sonya. Every minute of her life, Tania was answerable to her mom. She felt suffocated in her own house. The thought of going away to the hostel came as a respite, but that lasted momentarily.

Ramola had chosen a hostel which was even stricter. It was run by the Catholic community, and the nuns were a little too harsh on kids as far as discipline was concerned. It was here that Tania learned to pray in the chapel. She experienced a feeling of peace wash over her as she knelt before the Lord and prayed in moments of desolation. She prayed for Sonya too.

"Jesus replied, 'Love the Lord your God with all your heart and with all your soul and with all your mind.' Tania crossed her heart."

Tania and Sonya often met during their summer breaks. They caught up on their life's happenings in the absence of their mother. Sonya was always the understanding big sister that Tania missed having in life. During one of their recent homecomings in New Jersey, Tania observed that something had drastically changed in Sonya. She had become listless, kept to herself most of the time, and refused to come out of her room. There were dark circles beneath her eyes, signs that she was spending sleepless nights and kept popping pills. One day, Tania caught her drinking directly from their dad's Scotch bottle when Ramola was away.

"Sonya Di, is anything the matter?" Tania asked gently, handing her a cup of tea one morning.

Sonya smiled and turned away from her. She was trying hard to stop herself from crying, Tania noticed. These mood swings worried Tania, and she had asked her mom about it.

Ramola had rudely brushed away her worries. "You don't have to worry about Sonya. Focus on your life."

Tania knew things were not right with Sonya. Although her mom had kept the news of the rape attempt on Sonya hidden from her, she had come across it on social media. Why was mom not paying attention to Sonya? Why wasn't she taking her illness seriously?

Tania hugged herself tightly, afraid of loneliness. She did not want to end up like her sister. Tania felt a tremble begin in her legs, slowly spreading to her arms. She rubbed her palms together, but that did not stop the tremble that was fast spreading to the rest of her body. She rummaged through her handbag and removed a small packet. Her hands still shaking, Tania popped the dragonflies and washed them down with the coke laced with Vodka. She switched on the air pods, blasting music, switching out the world. A few seconds later, she felt ease wash over her. The inner turmoil she had experienced passed. Then Tania remembered an instance from the past.

Sonya was considerably agitated that morning as she paced in her room. Tania slowly crept in and closed the door.

"Di… Di… look what I got for you!" Sonya turned to find Tania holding a tiny packet with green capsules which she called, 'Dragonflies'.

"Di… trust me. This is the only solution to your problems." Tania's voice carried sincerity and genuine concern for her elder sister.

Sonya realised Tania was murmuring something under her breath.

"No temptation has seized you except what is common to man. And God is faithful; he will not let you be tempted beyond what you can bear. But when you are tempted, he will also provide a way out so that you can stand up under it."

"Who taught you to talk like this?" Sonya walked towards Tania, who was now looking at her with wide innocent eyes. Sonya, overwhelmed, gazed into her eyes, the same colour as hers, blue, like the sea, with big eyelashes curling upwards. The similarity ended there.

"Take it, Di... after all, we are humans who walk on the path shown to us by God," Tania said the words with finality as Sonya just stared at her in disbelief and then at the green capsule. Tania desperately wanted to help Sonya.

"Don't think much. I have been in and out on the threshold where you are standing now. You don't have much choice! If you want to survive, you've got to be tough."

Sonya was amazed at the maturity with which Tania spoke and overwhelmed by the love her sister exuded.

They were now sitting on the swing, looking at the sunset; Sonya's head leaning on Tania's shoulder. Sonya had calmed down considerably. Tania held onto her hand, comforting her through her moments of distress.

"I will always be here for you Di, always. I am as lonely as you. Help me Di,"

When Tania woke up, she was drenched in sweat. She realised she had been dreaming and calling out to Sonya.

Tania flung open the curtains. The sun was setting, but this sunset brought loneliness and despair to her mind. She was missing Sonya. She knelt and joined hands in a prayer. Rocking on her heels, Tania prayed fervently.

"So do not fear, for I am with you; do not be dismayed, for I am your God. I will strengthen you and help you; I will uphold you with my righteous right hand."

The verses she murmured, looking forlornly at the evening shadows. Her life among the nuns had restored a semblance of peace to her chaotic mind. Sending her to that college run by the nuns, was the only commendable thing her mom had done for her, she mused.

✻ ✻ ✻

Nandini waited patiently for Arjun in his cabin along with Maya. She wanted him to meet Maya. Although he didn't believe in shamanic practices, Nandini was adamant that the two meet up. She was prepared to face his wrath today.

A moment later, the cabin doors opened, and Arjun walked in followed by one of his subordinates. If he was surprised to see Nandini, he did not show it. Arjun threw a questioning glance at Maya, who appeared to be in a daze. She was sketching furiously in her notepad. Arjun dismissed his subordinate with a few signatures and took his chair.

"Hi Nandini … how have you been?", he was distracted by the stranger's presence and her weird behaviour.

"I'm good, Arjun…Umm…I wanted you to meet Maya."

Arjun's brows lifted in consternation.

Maya had finished sketching now and held it for Arjun to see. For a moment, Arjun was taken aback by what he saw. It was roughly a mirror image of Sonya's room.

Maya had a glassy look in her eyes. Arjun signalled Nandini to step aside.

"Has she been to Sonya's house? If she has, I can book her for trespassing," Arjun darted a suspicious look in Maya's direction.

"You still don't get it, do you?" Nandini asked, frustration obvious in her voice.

"This is the vision she has been having since Sonya's suicide, especially the closet in Sonya's bedroom," Nandini pointed to the sketch in his hands.

Arjun could feel her anger, but he needed to tread carefully.

"I understand my skills seem preposterous. It took me a while to understand what I possess is a gift and not a curse. But when non-believers like you question my special gift, I feel it's a curse," Maya turned to Arjun. She appeared exhausted but calm.

"Officer, I am just a medium for the souls who are waiting to crossover. I hope you understand there is no black magic involved here, no compulsion to put your belief in me," Maya steadied herself.

"Sonya wants you to look for something in her closet. It's not clear but I think she is guiding us in that direction," Maya's tone was sincere, and for a moment,

Arjun thought there was no wrong in checking Sonya's wardrobe.

Maya picked up her satchel. Before leaving, she handed a sketch to Arjun, who was shocked. Colour drained from his face.

Nandini saw him turn pale and walked over to him. She was looking at the sketch now. Arjun's expression had changed from shock to horror.

The sketch was that of a 10-year-old boy, peeking from behind his mother's pallu. He could see the fear in his eyes and apprehension as he stared ahead, presumably at his father's dead body that was missing in the sketch.

Arjun slumped down in the chair, overwhelmed by the sketch. These were his private thoughts, this was the horror he relived, again and again. He had not shared them with anyone, not even Nandini. Then how did this woman sketch it precisely? Was she for real? Arjun looked at her with disbelief.

Maya approached him. "I know this is unexpected, and I did not mean to shock you, just so I can prove myself." Maya's words were gentle. Arjun looked at her, still shocked.

"There are things in this world which are beyond our understanding."

Maya took a deep breath. "The moment I saw you, I could feel the inner turmoil you are going through. You are reliving the death of your father repeatedly in your mind. Let him go. Your father wants you to move on. He takes responsibility for his actions." Maya, saying so, started gathering her things.

Maya's words haunted him. His father wanted him to move on, but could he? Arjun needed to clear his father's name. He needed to clear the controversy surrounding his suicide. Arjun stared at the sketch, flabbergasted.

Nandini patted his shoulder comfortingly. Arjun shook his head in disbelief. He rubbed his eyes with the back of his palm.

"I don't know what to say. I am a non-believer in all this but…" He miraculously felt light as if a burden was lifted off his shoulders. He finally realised he could breathe freely.

Nandini wanted to reach out, comfort Arjun, but she knew she should wait, give him some time. Why was she feeling sad for this tough cop? To see him break like this was wrenching her heart, why?

When Arjun looked up, Maya had gone. He walked to where Nandini stood. He tapped her shoulder and was surprised to know she had been crying. Nandini went into his arms, sobbing and mumbling apologies.

"I had no intention of putting you through so much pain and grief," Nandini sobbed.

Arjun smiled down at Nandini, his fingers running through her hair. He took in the tangy scent as he turned her face towards him and gazed into her eyes. He so much wanted to kiss her upturned nose, feel her soft lips, and once again see her eyes twinkle as he kissed her.

"Don't ever go away. Stay… Nandini… stay… I need you," he mumbled, hugging her tighter. Taking Nandini in his arms seemed like the right thing to do.

Arjun held her at arm's length, his gaze caressing her face, and then he kissed her passionately. Nandini, for a moment, was taken by surprise.

"Nandini… I love you," Arjun murmured in her ear. Nandini glanced coyly at him.

"I love you too, Arjun." Nandini blushed, covering her face with her palms. Arjun took her in his arms and for a while neither spoke. Nandini, her head resting on his chest, was now toying with the buttons on Arjun's shirt.

Arjun raised her face towards him. His eyes travelled lovingly over her face, her flushed cheeks, and divine smile.

She looked questioningly at him, realising he wanted to say something.

"Nandini… I am sorry for not believing in you."

Nandini opened her mouth to say something but simply nodded.

"It's not your fault. Anyone else in your place… would have reacted in the same way. Just because we don't believe, doesn't mean it doesn't exist," Nandini said as Arjun let go of her and picked up the sketch from his desk.

"If what this woman says is true, then it's time to pay one more visit to Sonya's house."

Nandini touched his arm. "I am coming with you… please." They both walked out to the waiting police van. Vishwas joined them on the way out.

An eerie silence greeted them when the trio entered Sonya's apartment. Things were very much the same as he had left them on his last visit. He headed straight for Sonya's bedroom and could see the swing from the door, where they had found her blood-soaked body. The windows were shut, the blue and white lace curtains were still. Arjun and Nandini looked at each other, wondering if they were right about it.

"Sir, that's the closet from the sketch." Vishwas pointed to the closet and then to the sketch in his hands.

Arjun walked over to the closet and opened it. It was still unlocked. Arjun's men had gone through the contents of the closet in Ramola's presence, but they had not come across any secret compartment. He looked at Nandini, who threw him an anxious glance.

Sonya's clothes were neatly stacked in rows. Arjun and Vishwas emptied the closet to make the search easier. Arjun then ran his hands through the walls of the closet for any uneven surface. Suddenly, his fingers came across a gap between the drawer and the closet wall. Arjun pushed it gently, and a drawer shot open. Inside, they found a red leather-bound diary with Sonya's name inscribed in gold on its cover. There were also some letters stacked together between the pages. Arjun excitedly opened the diary. The letters he noticed were mailed from the US. He was aware that if it were not for Maya's vision, this diary would have gone unnoticed forever.

They were amazed as they went through the diary's contents. It had letters written by Sonya meant for Jay but never sent to him. It appeared as if Sonya was jotting down her day-to-day thoughts. It clearly showed how much Sonya was in love with Jay. There was one letter that caught Arjun's attention. It described Sonya and Jay's last meeting. Did it mean Sonya had already made up her mind to end her life when she went to see Jay?

Dear Jay,

When I came over to your office, I knew I was going to walk out of your life forever. I just needed to assure myself that what I was doing was right. I have chosen a path of self-destruction, and it is better you are not a part of it. Life for me is spiralling downwards. There is nothing much left to do now. I realised I end up hurting people I love.

I wanted to talk to you about Tania. She means the world to me. Tania is a very sweet girl. Sometimes I feel she is my mirror image. Mind and soul, we are the same. I would have loved to get to know her better, spend more time with her, spoil her rotten but things were never meant to happen that way. Mom kept both of us apart; reasons best known to her.

Jay, I want you to help Tania. Please support her and be a friend to her the way you have been to me. She is lonely. I have seen her eyes cloud with sadness. I am afraid she might walk the wrong path. You must help her. I have no one whom I can entrust her with.

Mom loves us lots but not the way we expect her to. Tania is doing drugs, and mom is unaware. I can't confide in mom because she will never understand and might even blame me for Tania's drug use. She does not trust me. When I tried telling her about Vikram abusing me, she did not so much as blink her eye! What can I expect from her? I do not want to lose Tania as she is family, the only one who loves me, cares for me, and understands me.

Jay, I love you and that one thing will never change. I have seen people around me whom I love abandon me. My birth mom abandoned me, walked out of my life. I met Meher while I was in US. I asked her why she brought me into this world! Now, when my life was upending, she wanted a part out of me. She tried to claim what was never hers. I would like to ask my dad why he stopped loving me. What does Ramola want from me? What can I do to be an ideal daughter? How can I make her love me? These questions will die with me.

Jay, life has handed me crap. I had not many expectations but whatever little I had ... I was robbed of all sanity.

Arjun paused, chewed on a thought aloud. "If we go by this letter, Sonya clearly holds Ramola responsible for things going wrong in her life. Ramola was planning to leave for the States the night Sonya committed suicide. She left Sonya alone in the house to deal with herself, taking Tania along with her. Ramola knew it was dangerous to leave Sonya alone as per Dr. Kulkarni's instructions." Arjun sighed. "Meher's letters showcase desperation. She thought she would waltz into Sonya's life and behave as if nothing happened."

"Sir, Ramola Rana kept many things from us, like Sonya being sexually abused as a child, her drinking problems, and now Tania's drug use as per Sonya's letter," Vishwas added.

"Sir, what I don't understand is, why put the blame for her daughter's death on Jay?" Vishwas's question set a chain of thoughts rolling in Arjun's mind.

"Ramola Rana wanted to distract us from the truth. She is buying time. Ramola had a bigger motive to push Sonya to the brink of her death."

There is a considerable level of ambiguity regarding Sonya's suicide. Jay happened to get caught in all this mess," Arjun stated.

Arjun turned to Vishwas. "Find out Tania's movements when Ramola and Sonya were in the States. It is time we call in the ladies for a formal chat. Before that happens, I need to check something."

"I knew this was not a simple suicide case from the very beginning," Nandini exclaimed, eyes twinkling with excitement and cheeks flushed.

Arjun smiled seeing the childlike excitement in Nandini.

"Maya's sketches further corroborated the facts, Arjun!" she squealed jubilantly.

Arjun agreed, nodding his head. "We were chasing the wrong person all this while. This letter, written by Sonya, proves it all." Arjun closed the diary, using the red silk thread as the marker.

Nandini was making notes. Arjun knew she was preparing a news report.

"Nandini, I do not want this leaked to the press … not yet. You will be the first to break the news, I promise," Arjun implored.

Nandini thought about it for a while, twirling the pen in her fingers as if considering Arjun's proposal, then she nodded her head.

"Fine… but I want to be present with you throughout the investigation of this case," Nandini raised her eyebrows to elicit a confirmation.

"Wherever it's permissible, I will take you along with me... promise." Arjun assured her as they walked out to the waiting van.

Ramola appeared to be in shock as Arjun told her they had found Sonya's diary in a secret compartment in her closet which says that Jay is innocent. Tania sat in the chair next to her, zoning in and out. She seemed unfazed, thought Arjun.

"How can it be possible? Jay is responsible for my daughter's death according to her letter, Mr. Deshmukh! Is this how you investigate a high-profile case?"

She no longer sounded confident. Still, Ramola was rude and arrogant.

Arjun was taken aback by the woman's audacity. From the very beginning, she had questioned the ability of his police force, and now she has the cheek to accuse them of shoddy investigation.

"Madam, every report pertaining to the case was considered and investigated. We have access to some new evidence. I need answers."

Ramola reluctantly nodded her head. She was curious about what new evidence the cop was talking about. They were sitting in the same, poorly lit room where Jay had been interrogated. Arjun knew he had fifteen minutes top before Ramola's lawyer showed up.

"Tell me the purpose of your trip to the States," Arjun was looking pointedly at her. He wanted answers and was confident this woman knew more than she was letting on.

"Yes… we did go to New Jersey to admit Sonya to psychiatric care. I asked Tania to come home as I was unable to persuade Sonya to go along." Ramola's voice wavered here. "Tania, why don't you say something?" Ramola nearly yelled at her daughter.

Arjun had wanted to interrogate Tania separately, but the girl seemed strange. It was better she had her mother for company.

"When mom called me in Canada, Sonya Di had locked herself in her room and refused to speak or meet anyone." Tania said. Ramola gave her a scathing look.

"Then what happened? Who convinced Sonya to go eventually?" Arjun questioned Tania.

"My mom says it happened right after Jay left her as he had failed in convincing Di to move to a psychiatric facility. By the time I reached home, it was eight days since Di had locked herself in her bedroom and refused to speak. When I reached home and called out to Di, she opened the door after lot of persuasion. She finally agreed to let us admit her to psychiatric care." Arjun noticed Tania spoke with no emotions. The voice was stable. There was no sign of grief on her face.

"Tania, as a child, were you aware of your uncle sexually abusing Sonya? Who else in the house knew about this?" At this question, Ramola threw back her chair and stood up.

"Tania is not answering that question. It has nothing to do with Sonya's suicide."

Ramola's eyes reflected anger, and did he notice a tinge of fear? Arjun thought.

"Dr. Kulkarni has already given his statement. The incidence of sexual abuse was one of the main reasons for Sonya's psychological breakdown. It aggravated in Singapore following the attempted rape by Mohan Kashyap."

"You must have spoken to Meher Rana, haven't you? It was she who abandoned her toddler daughter. Don't you think it left an indelible mark on the little girl's mind as she grew up?" Ramola's voice was laced with sarcasm and bitterness.

"You stepped in as Sonya's mother much before Tania was born. Your motherly love and care should have erased the pain the mother inflicted on the little girl. Don't you agree with me? We are not born with mental health issues. Most of the time, it's the circumstances and life experiences that break us down. Especially, people near to us are the cause of our downfall."

Arjun could see Ramola beginning to break down. She had no more defences left. His words had the desired effect. Sonya was Ramola's biggest defence, and she was no more now.

Ramola adjusted her dupatta, dabbed her eyes with a lace-embroidered kerchief.

"Where is my lawyer? He should have been here?" Ramola was upset at the turn of events. She darted a scathing look in Arjun's direction for accusing her.

"According to Dr. Kulkarni's statement, Sonya always had suicidal thoughts. Ramola Rana, you as her mother, know why."

"Not always... not always. My daughter was a very cheerful person... smiling, so full of life... in love." Ramola insisted.

"But her treating psychiatrist's opinion differs, Mrs. Rana," Arjun saw her wince. "According to Dr. Kulkarni, Sonya was going through severe depression stemming from childhood trauma and deception on the family's part." Arjun looked closely at Ramola to gauge her reaction.

Arjun noticed fleeting emotions on her face. First pain, then agitation, anxiety, and anger.

"He is bluffing. Sonya was full of lies," Ramola's voice was barely a whisper.

"Sonya was not bluffing. Why would she? Your brother Vikram abused your daughter while you chose to look the other way, Mrs. Rana," Arjun felt his temper rising, his body shook with anger as Sonya's face, as a little girl hurt and pained, flashed before his eyes.

Suddenly, Ramola turned to him, flashing anger. "You are conveniently trying to lay the blame for Sonya's death on me! Why do you want to save Jay?"

"Sonya was in love with Jay, but Jay used my daughter, exploiting her contacts," Ramola said, pain evident in her voice.

"Sonya was at the peak of her career when they fell in love. I never trusted him… not good enough for my daughter. Right from the beginning, I knew he spelled trouble." There was a sort of conviction in her voice.

"Maybe they were your overprotective, motherly feelings and worries!" Arjun commented in a sarcastic tone as Ramola gave him a look that said, "I know what I am talking about."

"I know who killed my daughter. It was not only Jay but this film industry whom she considered her family, their selfish attitude, their indifference towards her; they are all responsible for my daughter's death. They made her feel unwelcome. They gave up on Sonya." Ramola broke down crying.

Tania did not respond to her mother's sobs.

"Tania…" Arjun directed his next question to the girl who appeared to be in a stupefied state with what was going on around her.

"That fateful night, did Jay call to tell you that Sonya was alone at home and disturbed?"

Tania nodded. "Jay is telling the truth. He called but mom snatched the phone from my hands and asked him to stay out of our personal matter. She then sent me to my room." Tania didn't bother to look at Ramola who was giving her angry looks.

That evening was etched on Tania's memory forever.

"Tania… Tania, can you hear me?" Arjun was still calling out to her.

"Yes…sorry," Tania appeared disoriented.

She looked at Arjun and he could see her look hardening. Tania had once again shut herself.

"So, you are saying you didn't go to meet Sonya after a frantic call from Jay? It's hard to believe when you say that you loved your sister." Arjun was not ready to believe that Tania, who loved and cared for Sonya more than their mother, could leave her alone in such a state.

Tania was not beautiful or gorgeous like Sonya. Her round, cherubic face belied her age. She had a childlike innocence around her, observed Arjun. Was there envy towards her sister or a sense of competition in Tania? Though there was no resemblance between the stepsisters, they had the same eyes: sea-blue, deeply intense, and mysterious.

"Mom didn't want me to meet Sonya. Mom said, "I want to teach that rude, arrogant girl a lesson in her life. She is afraid of loneliness. She will know what loneliness feels like." Tania stated before withdrawing into a shell.

"Don't you think your behaviour towards your daughter, who is dealing with mental health issues, was harsh and insensitive?' Arjun could feel his blood boil.

"This is a half-truth. I must have said something to that effect but did not mean it. Sonya asked me to leave. She wanted to be left alone. You don't understand how difficult it is to handle a person like Sonya, who is so volatile." Ramola was distraught.

"We always go out of our way for the people we love. You say you loved Sonya, but you didn't even let her enjoy being Tania's big sister. Were you afraid of losing Tania? Arjun's question caused Ramola to wince. He noticed a nerve began to twitch on her forehead.

"I had my own reasons to keep them apart. That doesn't mean I ill-treated or instigated my daughter to end her life. A mother has a right and a say over her children. My upbringing has not played a part in how Sonya turned out. It was the people around her in professional life that gave up on her. I never gave up on my daughter... never would..." Ramola said in one breath.

Partly it was true, agreed Arjun to himself. Most of the time it was the social conditions that played an important part in a person's life, but somewhere down the line, their loved ones are also responsible for the emotional and psychological upheavals going on in one's mind. There were social reasons behind my father's suicide, but we as his family had failed him too.

"Di was disturbed throughout. It seemed she had built a wall around her. It felt like Di had... given up."

"Why do you think Jay was responsible for Sonya's suicide?" The question was directed at them both. Tania was about to answer, but Ramola gave her a sharp glance.

"I am quite sure that it was Jay who drove my daughter to commit suicide," Ramola said firmly.

"Sonya does not hold Jay responsible for her death." The finality with which Arjun said this startled Ramola. Tania looked confused.

"What do you mean by that? Those letters written by Sonya do prove that Jay used her, and she was hurt," Ramola replied angrily.

"That is your misconception, Mrs. Rana. When a person is hurting inside, we tend to find someone to vent our anger on. I am not defending Jay. The law will take its own course." Saying this, Arjun withdrew the red leather-bound diary he had found in Sonya's closet.

"I hope you recognise the writing. This diary belongs to Sonya, and it even has her name engraved on its cover," Arjun said, handing it to Ramola.

"Where did you find this? I had no idea Sonya was writing a diary. Did you, Tania?" Ramola looked at Tania, who also shook her head in denial.

Arjun ignored Ramola's question. "Madam, if you go through its contents, you will find your daughter has written this diary as a one-way dialogue with Jay. These letters were never meant to be sent to Jay. It was Sonya's way of communicating with Jay, whom she loved deeply as you can make out from its contents. I have marked a page, which is the last entry written by Sonya before she committed suicide. She came across as mentally disturbed."

Ramola was shocked by this revelation. She stared wide-eyed at the diary. Slowly, still dazed, she opened the page and started reading it.

There was surprise, shock, pain, and then a feeling of being let down reflected on Ramola's face as she flicked through the pages. Arjun was familiar with that feeling.

The feeling of desertion, isolation, and rejection that carried pain and misery, leaving you hurting for the rest of your life.

"Did you know Sonya was in touch with Meher, her birth mother?"

Ramola was flabbergasted at this revelation. She looked at Tania, who averted her gaze.

"You knew…? What else have you been hiding from me?" Ramola angrily questioned Tania.

There was a knock on the door. Pawar peeped in, signalling the arrival of the lawyer. Arjun nodded in acknowledgement.

"One last question, Ramola Rana." Arjun pushed a file towards Ramola. Her eyes widened in fear.

"What are you trying to prove by showing me this file, Officer?"

"These are Sonya's life insurance papers, and these are the papers for your bungalow in New Jersey. It says here that Sonya has transferred her rights to you."

Ramola tried to put up an act of indifference.

"Isn't the timing just perfect? A month before, Sonya committed suicide." Arjun pressed on.

"Is it a crime to insure a daughter's life, Officer? Tania also has a life insurance policy. Does it mean I am planning to kill her?" Ramola scoffed.

"Don't you think the amount insured is insanely high? 50 crores? The nominee listed here is yourself, Ramola Rana. Very smart."

"What about the papers transferring the house to you?"

Before Ramola could reply, the doors were thrown open, and Advocate Saxena stormed in.

"My clients will not answer any more questions. I am here to take them home." He waved some legal papers at him.

Arjun raised his hands in a gesture of surrender. Ramola had a victorious smile on as she shepherded Tania out of the interrogation room, accompanied by Advocate Saxena.

Tania was about to get into the car when she felt a hand grip her arm. She looked quizzically at the woman who was now handing her a paper. She whispered something in Tania's ear. Aghast and speechless, Tania turned to the paper the woman had stuck in her hands. It was a sketch.

✳ ✳ ✳

"We live in strange times, Arjun. Anything can be possible! Pigs can fly!" CP Sahay sighed and offered Arjun tea, taking one cup for himself. They were now sitting across from each other in Sahay's sprawling cabin.

Arjun had briefed the senior cop about Sonya Rana's suicide case. First, it was hard to believe that Ramola Rana, to save herself, could keep the 'abuse' part a secret, hidden even from Sonya's therapist!

Sahay rubbed his chin, lost in deep thought. "Hard to believe a mother can be capable of all that."

"Stepmother," Arjun added, showing him the sketches Maya had drawn for them. Sahay looked at him quizzically.

"This is from Maya, the mystical lady. I thought it would do no harm bending a little towards the paranormal."

When Arjun looked up, he saw a strange look pass over Sahay's face, inquisitive.

"Who's the girl?" Now it was Arjun's turn to be surprised.

"Go on, tell me. Who is she? A person in love tends to take risks." Sahay patted Arjun's back, lit a cigar and took a puff.

Arjun smiled and knew he was blushing. "Nandini. She is a journalist..." Sahay was grinning now. "And before you get anything more in your head, Nandini believes in Maya, so..."

"So, you thought it wouldn't do any harm to place your trust in Maya," Sahay completed the sentence for Arjun, who gestured his lips were sealed.

"All right, jokes apart, this lady, Maya, sure has mystical powers. She has been a great help to the department. Now listen very carefully… keep this between us. We've got to protect Maya's identity. Don't utter a word about her to anyone."

Sahay glanced at the sketches. "Unbelievable."

"Sonya's diary helped Jay get bail. Soon his case will be dismissed. Do you still think it was suicide?"

Arjun looked thoughtful at the questions raised by the senior cop.

"As for now, I have no option but to rule it as a suicide, giving Sonya's mental condition, and Dr. Kulkarni's statement." Arjun said.

"Judgement is passed based on evidence. It is going to be difficult to prove Ramola Rana is guilty," Sahay pondered on the thought, taking a puff at the cigar. "Also, there is Meher Rana, who abandoned Sonya as a toddler. Then, the father marries Ramola Rana, whose brother sexually abused little Sonya. Not believing and acknowledging that your child is being sexually abused is convenient for the adults. It messes up the victim's psyche."

"Majority of the times it is a close member of family who sexually abuses the kid," Sahay sighed as he swivelled his chair to face Arjun, who was staring out at the calm sea.

"Do you know what I am thinking at this point?" Arjun turned to Sahay, who had a look mixed with curiosity and anticipation. It had always been a wonder to watch the younger cop work, unearth crime, and solve tricky cases.

"What do you call a person who has everything but is still unhappy from within? I call him unfortunate. You know what's scary about this whole case?" Arjun looked pointedly at Sahay and said, aiming to drive his point home.

"This case has many loopholes, and it has left me with doubts. I somewhere feel that Tania had something to do with Sonya's death." Arjun scratched his head; confident he was right.

"What does Tania have to do with her sister's suicide? She has been denied the happiness of having a sister despite having one throughout her life. Imagine loving and caring for your sister in secret. The poor girl has turned to drugs and found solace in an alternative religion."

It looked like Arjun did not agree with Sahay as he shook his head.

"What exactly happened to plant that seed in your mind?" Sahay trusted a cop's intuition and believed it could never be in vain.

"I am amazed at Tania's resilience. The sisters were inseparable. Sonya's death doesn't seem to have affected Tania. She is calm as if she was expecting Sonya to die."

"Remember, I described the crime scene to you? I am still not convinced," Arjun stressed on the last words.

"The way her body was positioned. It was as if she was laid to rest. Sonya was not alone that fateful evening. Someone was with her in that room, I am sure... but who?" Arjun narrowed his eyes, thought lines etching his forehead.

"These questions will do you no good. Let the dead be," Sahay patted his back.

"You can never fully understand a person or judge a relationship. Many times, what we see is just a cover pulled over to hide our vulnerability. My advice to you, young lad: do not go down the rabbit hole."

Arjun sighed as he looked at Sahay. He realised the man had grown old. His father would have been of the same age as him. If his father was alive, would he have been having this same conversation?"

"I warned you about not going down the rabbit hole, didn't I?"

Arjun held the senior cop's hand and gazed lovingly at him.

"You are all the family I have left." Arjun's eyes became moist.

Sahay nodded. "Sometimes I feel family is too imposing... dangerous. They control your life," Sahay moved the empty teacups. He took a new cigar and put it to his mouth. He was about to light it when Arjun took away the lighter from his hand.

"See what I mean!" Sahay rolled his eyes at Arjun and put the cigar away.

"Family or no family... a man has very few choices," Sahay sat back in his chair, sighing.

"I have handed in my resignation." Arjun looked quizzically at the senior cop.

"Don't give me that shocked look! A man deserves to spend some quality time for himself. I have had enough of murders, terror attacks, red tape and bureaucracy. I want to retire and live a peaceful life, on an island with my Zach," Sahay had a dreamy look in his eyes.

"You are deserting me, don't you think? I still need some answers from you," Arjun had that no-nonsense look on his face, and Sahay knew he better not test the latter's patience. It was time to cough up some answers.

Sahay walked to his cabinet and pulled out a cardboard box. He placed it on his desk and turned to Arjun, who looked mystified.

He pointed towards it. "Your father left it for you. It's yours, and I hope you find answers to the questions that have been haunting you. I had been planning to give this to you all the while... I think I was waiting for the right moment."

Sahay patted the young cop's shoulder and finally got around to light another cigar. He stood at the window, overlooking the sea, taking a long drag, leaving Arjun to figure out his past.

For five minutes, Arjun just stared at the box as if waiting for it to spring open on its own. Hands trembling, he opened the box and found a bundle wrapped in satin cloth. He gingerly opened it and to his surprise found some old photographs. The first few were of his dad with his colleagues. There were a couple of them with Sahay in happier times. There was one picture with a man a little older than his father. Arjun tried hard to recollect who he was but failed to do so. He racked his brains, thinking hard if he had found any mention of this man in many of his conversations he had with his mother until she passed away after a brief illness.

So engrossed was Arjun that he did not realise the senior cop standing next to him.

"It's high time you met someone." Sahay picked up his jacket and motioned Arjun to follow him.

They were standing outside a bungalow located in the far suburbs of Mumbai. Sahay wanted to light another cigar, but he thought better and raised the bar off the old iron gate. It creaked painfully like an old man's bones, its sound reverberating in the afternoon stillness. Arjun looked at the senior cop quizzically, but Sahay maintained his silence and instead walked to the main door.

Sahay looked around and knocked the brass knob on the wooden door. A few minutes must have passed before the door was opened by a middle-aged lady. She had a matronly look about her. From the way she smiled, it was evident she knew Sahay. No one said a word as they were led into the quaint living room.

Sahay was sweating as he loosened his tie. The woman offered them cool lemonade, and they thankfully gulped it down. A few more minutes of this silence, and Arjun's patience had started to wear off. He felt he was part of dumb charades.

"Could you care to explain why you have dragged me here in this sweltering heat?" Arjun spoke under his breath.

"You will soon know. Don't be so impatient. Acquiring knowledge before time can be hazardous!" Sahay rolled his eyes and puffed his cheeks.

"Who says so?" Arjun asked as Sahay jabbed a finger in his chest.

"Thought as much… stop throwing bookish lines at me." Arjun dabbed beads of sweat off his forehead.

Arjun started pacing the room, taking in its interiors. It was an old bungalow, no doubt. Paint had chipped off in corners. There was water seepage somewhere in the other room as the ceiling in the hall had wet patches. Arjun noticed the walls were once painted a canary yellow but now had faded with time. His ears perked up at the scraping sound from outside the door. Arjun looked at Sahay, who had braced himself for whoever was approaching them.

A frail old man was wheeled into the room by the same woman who had let them in. Arjun recognised him from the photographs he had seen a while ago. The only difference being the man had aged considerably. He had silver hair, wisps flying around his face, his eyebrows too had greyed with age and wrinkles etched on his face. Arjun noticed the tremble in the old man's right hand and leg and the lips twitching. He must have suffered a paralytic stroke on the right side of his body, he concluded. Arjun darted a glance at Sahay, who seemed wary. Delving into past was not the senior cop's fortitude.

Arjun darted an anxious glance at Sahay, signalling for introductions. Sahay cleared his throat and got up from his chair.

"Sir ... I want you to meet someone." Sahay said, now standing very close to the old, wizened man. He just rolled his eyes up at him and nodded his head.

Sahay pointed in Arjun's direction. "He is Arjun Manohar Deshmukh. You remember Manohar…" At this, the old man stopped Sahay with a wave of his hand. He motioned for Arjun, who approached him warily.

They were now sitting in the small garden that the two had passed on their way in. The housekeeper had arranged for tea and snacks, but Arjun was too nervous to touch anything. He had so many questions about his father that he needed answered! A wave of curiosity was building up within him, gathering momentum like hundreds of horses, thudding to the finish line. The only difference was their finishing line was marked, but Arjun's life's momentum depended on what the man was about to reveal.

The old man turned to Arjun and stared at him.

"My name is Chandrakant Rai. I headed the Covert Encounter Wing of the Maharashtra Police, and your father assisted me. He was a brave and noble officer." He spoke with great difficulty.

"If he was brave, why did he commit suicide like a coward?" Arjun, for the first time, realised he had so much anger boiling in his heart.

Sahay was about to reprimand him, but Chandrakant stopped him, shaking his head 'no.'

"Everything in life is painted in vivid colours. If this world were black or white, imagine how boring life would have been!" Chandrakant wiped the saliva from his lips and replaced the napkin back on his lap, hands trembling.

Arjun looked quizzically at him, trying to understand what the old man was attempting to say.

"Every person is different and reacts differently to various circumstances. We can't hold anything against them. He was your father. Try to understand him. It is not easy to give up everything... not easy."

Arjun still appeared unconvinced. Chandrakant had a faraway look in his eyes as he narrated the tragic incident that took place one fateful evening.

"I, your father and a few officers were following a dreaded underworld criminal. We had orders to shoot on sight. We gave chase, and suddenly the gangster entered a forest area. Daylight was fast fading, and we had little time and hope of catching him." The man became breathless at this point. Sahay got up to help him, but he raised his finger and motioned for him to remain seated.

He took in deep breaths and then said, "Your father wanted to catch him alive, but I was opposed to the idea. I wanted to kill him at any cost. Your father had faith in the Indian judiciary system." Chandrakant sighed, once again wiped the saliva from his lips, and turned to look at Arjun, who was listening intently. His life depended on it.

"After an hour-long chase, we were able to corner him, and suddenly he opened fire at us. I was in the gangster's line of fire. Your father had a clear shot but despite signalling him to shoot, he refused and slowly started edging towards him, in the hope of capturing him alive! Suddenly, there were a few more shots, and I realised I was hit. I took two bullets; one in my stomach and the other pierced my spine." Chandrakant pointed to where the bullet had entered and exited through his spine.

"I noticed, Manohar had managed to disarm the gangster and handcuff him. He was bundled into the waiting police van."

Chandrakant took a deep breath, swatting a fly off his immobile leg.

"Then what happened?" Arjun was getting impatient. He had shifted to the edge of his chair. Sahay patted his hand comfortingly.

"The gangster was let off eventually for want of evidence. Some big people rallied around him, and he escaped abroad. I became paralysed from the waist down. Manohar blamed himself for my handicap and slowly slipped into depression.

He was reprimanded by our seniors for not following orders and suspended." The old cop now looked at Arjun, who had a faraway look in his eyes.

"Do you hold my father responsible for what happened to you?" Arjun asked, pain etched in his voice.

Chandrakant's pupils were a shade of ash black. Arjun noticed. "Your father did what he believed was right. What followed later were a chain of unfortunate events. Manohar being the emotional kind... took it to his heart and..." Chandrakant's words trailed off as he leaned back in his chair, exhausted.

Arjun stared after the old man as he was wheeled inside the house. He felt the burden of his heavy past slip off his shoulders. He slumped down in the chair, relief washing over him.

Arjun felt Sahay comforting him, patting his shoulder. "Chandrakant was away in London all these years. Last month, I received a call from his son. He said Chandrakant wanted to come home to take care of urgent work here."

Sahay lit a cigar which he had been aching to have until now and took a drag, staring ahead.

"I was surprised when Chandrakant asked to meet me. It was then that I told him about you, and he insisted on seeing you. The rest is history," Sahay swept his hands in a gesture, "you-know-it-all."

Arjun stood up to face Sahay. "Thanks for everything." He took the cigar from Sahay's lips, threw it on the ground amid Sahay's protests, and stomped on it.

"Don't look so crestfallen. I know you will light another one. Let's go…" Arjun walked towards the gate, feeling the weight lift off his shoulders.

* * *

The room resembled one big chaos, as if a hurricane had turned the closet inside out. Tees, shirts, denims, shorts all lay strewn on the bed in a haphazard pile. More clothes flew from the closet as Jay rummaged through his drawers and at the same time called out for his mom.

"Mom… mom… I need you to help me with my packing… mom…" Jay shouted at the top of his voice, adding more clothes to the pile on the bed.

Sandhya hurried into the room and for a moment froze at the mess her son had created.

"Jay… Oh my God! What have you done? What is this mess!" she exclaimed, beginning to fold the clothes and sort them out one by one.

Jay wrung his hands in despair and turned to her. "Mom… I am confused about what clothes I should take with me. It's going to be chilly out there. I need formals for the presentation and some casual stuff too." Jay looked around at the mess and pulled at his hair.

"Mom… please, you decide what I should be taking with me. Don't involve me…" Saying this, Jay picked up his cell phone and began checking for messages while Sandhya looked at him exasperated.

It was a week since Jay was released on bail. Sandhya and Rishabh had sensed the change in their son. He had not uttered Sonya's name. If he happened to hear it in news or come across a post on social media, he would skip it.

Rishabh knew Jay was hurting inside, and he did not want to expose Jay to any insensitive talks or statements. The day Jay was let out on bail, Rishabh and Sandhya led him out through the rear entrance of the courtroom, bundled him into their car, and took him to their farmhouse in Karjat to avoid the paparazzi on their trail.

Jay was preparing to leave for Delhi. Their agency had secured an important contract, and they needed to discuss terms and conditions before they closed the deal.

Jay absentmindedly walked to the terrace adjoining his bedroom and sat down on one of the chairs, engrossed in deleting the unwanted messages from his cell phone. He was taken by surprise upon coming across a backdated voice message from Sonya. His body tensed, hands trembled.

His finger lingered for a moment on the delete button as he contemplated the next step of action.

Sonya's death had wrought anguish and despair to Jay. He was not given a chance to mourn her death or weep for the loss. He wanted to meet Ramola aunty and share her grief, cry on her shoulders, and share fond memories of Sonya with her, but instead, he was unceremoniously sent to prison for no fault of his.

Jay swiped away the tears with the back of his hand and once again looked at the message icon, feet tapping. This message must have somehow escaped the scrutiny of the police.

Sweat trickled down his brow as his finger danced on the delete button. Since the day he came home, Jay had promised himself he would put everything behind him and move on in life. Now, he shook off the heaviness that seemed to fill his head and pressed the "ON" button, putting his cell on speaker mode. Sonya's sweet voice rang through the sunny afternoon.

"Jay... when you listen to this message, I shall have travelled far away from you... from your world. Throughout my life, my soul has wandered in search of peace but found only turmoil within. Your love soothed my frayed nerves but the moment I pushed you away, I felt distraught. I was hurting inside. I was trying to protect

you, baby. The more I put distance between us, the more I yearned for you. At last, I realised, it's difficult to find peace in love."

Jay paused the audio and restlessly paced around the terrace. He couldn't bear to hear her cry... hear her voice filled with sadness. He clutched his stomach, and doubled down, sobbing and choking.

"I loved you, Sonya... wish you had given me a chance... us a chance. I loved you... I loved you... I loved you..." Unknown to Jay, he let go of the pause button and Sonya started speaking again.

"My birth was not my choice nor my life, but there was one thing that was in my hands... my death. No one can take it away from me... not even God. Goodbye Jay."

Jay astounded, stared at the cell phone dumbfounded. He took in a deep breath, walked over to the balcony, and flung the cell phone as far as he could. He watched it hurtle down to the road below until it was just a dot, a grim reminder of his past.

Jay wiped the tears and took in a deep breath. The past few months had hardened him to face life in a new light. Sonya was his beautiful past, a memory which will remain with him. He had decided not to grieve for her when it was proved in the court that Sonya's death was by suicide. It was her decision to go, and he respected it.

He stepped into his bedroom and hugged his mom. Sandhya didn't have to see his face to know that he had cried. She patted his hand.

"Mom... Please ask Gullu to keep my bags in the car. I have to send out an email. And mom...I need a new cell phone and..."

There was hope and newfound enthusiasm in Jay's voice.

Six Months Later

The empty swing in the backyard of their house in New Jersey reminded Tania of good times with Sonya. They had spent many evenings together, swinging, staring at the blue sky above, listening to birds chirping in the trees, the wind buzzing through the trees... the two of them did not really have to speak a word. They understood each other and found solace in the silence their company provided.

Tania remembered how, as a child, she would tag behind Sonya Di, urging her to carry her, put her on the slide, share chocolates, or simply take her for a ride on her bicycle. She had a vivid memory of Di holding both her hands and twirling her round and round; the trees, the mountains fading into a hazy blur, the sounds morphing into one, and the childish giggles filling up any dull afternoon.

Sonya, the adventurous sort, had taken Tania to the mountaintop. Tania, afraid of heights, had resisted at first. However, when Sonya sat her on the bicycle and cycled through the woods, Tania immediately felt at ease and knew she was safe with Di next to her.

Sonya had then pointed to the highest mountain and said, "Tania, someday I want to climb that mountain. I know I will."

Tania had simply nodded her head, believing her Di could do the impossible.

Tania brushed away dope-induced drowsiness from her eyes and sat down on the swing … its joints creaking. They need to be oiled, she mused. It was a Sunday activity with dad. Sonya would carry a tiny oil can, and Tania would watch; their father would pour little drops onto the joints to relieve them of any rust.

"Hardly anyone comes here now, though", thought Tania, taking a swig from the bottle. She had fond memories of her childhood and always felt connected to this house.

Tania remembered their last visit home. Sonya was strolling in the garden, lost in thoughts. Suddenly, she would stop, look around, as if expecting someone to jump at her. Tania could make out an unknown fear in her eyes, and it pained her.

"Di… is anything wrong?" Tania would hold her hand, offering warmth and comfort, and Sonya's blue eyes darted around in fear.

Sonya would whisper back, her eyes darting furtively around, "I feel like someone is watching me… following me. They can hurt us, Tania."

"There is no one here, Di… let's sit on the swing for old times' sake." The swing was the only place where Sonya felt a level of comfort and homecoming, Tania knew.

Tania offered her the green pills, which Sonya gulped down with the Scotch she was nursing. Later, they sat on the swing, Sonya's head resting on Tania's shoulder. Everything else faded: the chirping of the birds, the wind in the trees, the crashing waves… it was just the two of them.

Sonya lay down on the swing, her head in Tania's lap. The swing had slowed down, creaking sounds magnified by the afternoon silence. After a while, Sonya stirred awake and sighed.

"Tania… I want you to promise me… don't hold me back… ever…when it is the time"

Tania did not reply, instead she stared at the mountain that her Di so much wanted to climb and without saying a word took Sonya's hand in hers and gave it a gentle squeeze.

Tania looked at the sketch Maya had handed her. It showed a girl on the balcony, her gaze horrified at something she was seeing.

"Come to me, all you who are weary and burdened, and I will give you rest."

That night when Tania let herself into the house with a spare key, despite her mother's admonishments, she could hear Sonya sobbing. She hurried over to Sonya and was shocked at seeing the knife in her hands. Tania without giving it a thought, rushed towards Sonya thinking she would snatch the knife from her. But before she could do anything, Sonya had slashed her wrist, repeatedly with the knife, causing blood to gush out.

"Tania … you promised…please." Sonya was finding it hard to breathe.

Tania placed Sonya's head in her lap and soothed her hair, patting her forehead, kissing her, and comforting her in her last moments. Tania was sobbing, panicking at what her sister wanted her to do. How could she let her sister die? This was a much bigger decision. But then she realised that Sonya, her entire life, had fought hard not to survive. Everyone around her had let her down, eventually. Being her sister and her only friend, she was not going to let her down.

The wind carried the paper through the trees and to the mountains beyond. Tania now sprawled on the swing, taking in the blue of the skies, the green of the trees, humming a song from their childhood. A fond smile graced her face. She had fulfilled Sonya's wish. She had set her sister free.

* * *

The house that Meher and Raghav once called their own stood desolate and empty, a haunting shell of memories. This was the very place where Sonya was born, only to be cruelly abandoned by her birth mother. Within these walls, the innocent girl endured unspeakable horrors, subjected to sexual abuse and left shattered, with no one to help her piece together her fractured spirit. Yet, paradoxically, this was also the sanctuary where two sisters discovered a profound love for one another. Brick by brick, they reconstructed their lives, gathering their broken selves in a courageous effort to forge a semblance of normalcy amidst the chaos.

Though they shared the same father, an invisible thread of connection seemed absent between them. Little did they realise, however, that a powerful similarity bound them—an undercurrent of shared insanity. This unique bond allowed them to comprehend each other's primal and psychological needs, intertwining their fates irrevocably.

This very house bore witness to the trials and tribulations of the Rana family. It was the battleground where a tempest named Ramola stormed in, irrevocably altering the destiny of the innocent girl who found herself ensnared in darkness. The echoes of their struggles lingered in the air, a testament to resilience and the complexity of love amidst suffering.

Ramola noticed her daughter was relaxed and happy after a long time. The night Sonya died, she had followed Tania home and found her on the swing with Sonya's head in her lap. For a moment, Ramola skipped a heartbeat. She thought Tania was hurt. She shook Tania, who started sobbing hysterically. There was Sonya's blood on her clothes. Ramola didn't even bother to check for a pulse on Sonya. Instead, she began to drag Tania away when Ramola noticed Sonya open her eyes and raise her hand towards her. Was it a plea for help? Ramola would never know as she stood her ground, staring at Sonya, who breathed her last.

The skies were exceptionally clear for a cloudy day, as predicted by the weather department. The forbidding times were past them. The despair that had cast its shadow on their family ended with Sonya's death. Ramola made a drink for herself and logged into her bank account. She grinned at the figures that jumped out at her. Sonya had been generous in death. Ramola booked a cruise holiday for herself and Tania. Gleefully, she finished the drink and poured herself another. Ramola looked around at the cartons, which were packed and ready to be disposed of.

These were parts of her sordid past that she didn't want to carry with her. Ramola had sold the house and was moving into a bigger house in San Francisco. She had plans for Tania. Now, with Sonya gone, she could focus on Tania. The thought calmed her.

Ramola's gaze wandered to the main gate, and she noticed a woman standing across the street, staring at her. For a moment, she thought it was Sonya. The glass slipped from her hand as Ramola ran to the front door and threw it open, hoping against hope it was slight of the eye. To her relief, there was no one there. It could be a passing stranger, she assured herself.

The kitchen door opened, and Tania walked in. Ramola noticed something in her daughter's hand. At the questioning look from her mother, Tania opened her palm, setting the dragonfly free.

"Will you ever grow up? Help me load the bags in the car. I am dying to get out of this forsaken place." Ramola mumbled the last bit to herself.

"We are giving ourselves a new start. I hope everything works out. Change will do you good." Ramola started the car and drove off. Tania already had her air pods tuned in, music blasting from the cell phone and her mother's voice tuned out.

They didn't notice their fellow traveller, the dragonfly on the rear windshield of their car.

* * *

Meher had seen Ramola and Tania drive away. She entered the house through the garden gate. The girl must have left it open by mistake, thought Meher. She sat on the swing and broke down. The last time she met Sonya was in the theatre. Since then, Sonya's words haunted her.

"Did you ever, for a moment, love me? Was there a time in your life that you regretted abandoning me?"

Meher was everything but a liar. She still remembered Sonya's dejected look when Meher kept her silence.

She had failed her daughter. She had killed her daughter because of one reckless decision born out of selfishness.

Acknowledgement

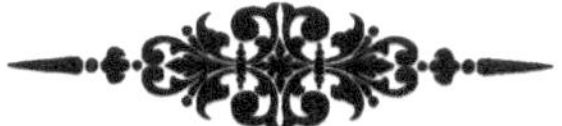

It takes a tribe to raise a village, and it takes a dedicated group of people to create a book. I have been fortunate to have many wonderful individuals by my side throughout the creation of **Dragonflies**.

I extend my heartfelt gratitude to Dr. Sumedha Tiwari, a neuropsychiatrist, for sharing her expertise on the clinical scenes in the book.

A big thank you to Jasreet Kaur Bachhal, my publishing manager at Notion Press. She has been the guiding force at every step, right from the beginning to the completion of this project. You are my hero, Jasreet.

Thank you, Tika Rai, for designing the most stunning book cover. Huge thanks to my wonderful editor, Dainty Wellington, who patiently tolerated all my whims and incorporated every minute change I made to the manuscript. I also appreciate Murali Pandian for his aesthetic design of the book's interior.

Thank you to Bhavana, Content Marketing Specialist; Kishore Kumar, Digital Marketing Specialist; and Vidhyalakshmi, Senior Digital Marketing Strategist at Notion Press.

A special thanks to Swetha at Notion Press, who diligently explained the entire publishing process. She is instrumental in convincing me to place my trust in Notion Press and I am glad I did.

This book would not be complete without mentioning my daughter, Priyanka, a crusader for mental health. Having faced her own challenges, she has emerged as a strong advocate. I am also grateful to my husband, Raju Parulekar, for his unwavering support of my passion for writing and for putting up with my mood swings.